DR. YEN SIN:
THE MYSTERY OF THE DRAGON'S SHADOW

THE INVISIBLE PERIL
DR. YEN SIN™

THE MYSTERY OF THE
DRAGON'S SHADOW

By Donald E. Keyhoe

ALTUS PRESS • 2016

EDITED AND DESIGNED BY

Matthew Moring

PUBLISHING HISTORY

"The Mystery of the Dragon's Shadow" originally appeared in the May/June, 1936
  (Vol. 1, No. 1) issue of *Dr. Yen Sin* magazine. Copyright 1936 by Popular Publica-
  tions, Inc. Copyright renewed 1963 and assigned to Steeger Properties, LLC. All
  rights reserved.

CHAPTER 1
THE MAN WHO NEVER SLEPT

FOG, LIKE a sinister cloak, had swept in from the Potomac, enshrouding Washington in its clammy folds. By nine o'clock, the Capital lay buried under an ocean of drifting mist, the lights of Pennsylvania Avenue only blurred yellow spots in the almost impenetrable gloom.

Unseen cars crawled along the famous thoroughfare, the hoarse blasts of their horns muffled in the evil-smelling murk. Shadowy forms moved like phantoms in the fog.

But there was one shadow which did not move.

Almost invisible in the blackness of a shop-entry, stood a motionless figure. Except for its low, harsh breathing, it might have been a dummy—a wooden figure placed there to draw attention to the trinkets in the window. But the window was dark, and the shop was closed.

Minutes passed, and still the shadow did not move. There was something more than ominous about that crouching form. It was as though Death itself lurked there in the fog, inexorably waiting.

Just once, the man's arm lifted. For an instant, blurred light from the nearby restaurant fell on a dark-skinned hand, on a curious silken noose gripped between powerful fingers. Then the hand was jerked back, and the strangler's cord was swiftly hidden from view....

A bone cracked and the Burman thug dropped to the sidewalk.

HARDLY A hundred feet away, within the picture-paneled walls of the Restaurant Occidental, two men lingered over their coffee. Both would have drawn a second glance, though they were totally different. One was very tall, with a lean, tanned face and dark-brown, restless eyes. Something about him seemed

to belie the conventional garb of his smartly tailored sack suit. His deep-burned tan gave hint of wanderings in far-off places. He had the look of a man who has lived keenly—but who has traveled alone.

His companion was somewhat shorter; with a compact build which just escaped being chunky. His blond hair was rumpled, as though to hide its slight tendency to wave, and his blue eyes held an engaging, almost boyish frankness. He took a pipe and a tobacco pouch from the pocket of his white linen coat, and as he carelessly filled the briar he looked across the table, his ruddy face lit with a genial grin.

"You know, Michael, you're a puzzle—if you don't mind my saying so on this short acquaintance."

Even a careful observer would not have caught the sudden flicker in Michael Traile's dark eyes, the swiftly concealed reaction of a man at once on his guard.

"I'm afraid you're looking for mysteries, Eric," he said with a whimsical smile. "Isn't that Department of Justice teletype affair enough of a problem?"

Eric Gordon nodded, emphatically. "Plenty—and that's another thing. How'd you learn so much about teletype circuits?"

Traile glanced at the blue smoke curling up from his cigarette. "It was just an accident, my spotting that point."

Eric bit down hard on the stem of his pipe. "Accident nothing! You showed me more in a day than the company experts taught me in a month. And then the Bureau of Investigation chief comes out and says it's only one of your hobbies. He bet me I could name any ten subjects and you'd be up on nine of them."

Traile grinned quizzically. "So that's the reason for this devious conversation."

"Yes, and I've lost twenty bucks," Eric growled. "How the devil was I to know you were a walking encyclopedia?"

A briefly bitter expression crossed the other man's bronzed face.

"Oh, Lord, I didn't mean it that way," exclaimed Eric, contritely. "I was just wondering how you ever packed so much into one life without being twins. You can't be more than four years older than I am, but you act—I mean you seem to know as much as if you'd—" He floundered for a moment, his boyish face as red as a poppy. "Maybe some day I'll learn to keep my mouth shut," he ended savagely.

The bitter light faded from Traile's eyes. "It's all right, old man. You just happened to touch a sensitive spot. A peculiar circumstance has forced me to dabble in many things—in fact, has controlled my entire life."

He hesitated, seemed about to go on, then abruptly squashed out his cigarette and motioned to the waiter. Eric's blue eyes held a bewildered look as he followed the taller man to the door. But Traile's face had become an inscrutable mask. At the entrance he paused to put on his Panama. He glanced at Eric Gordon's bare head.

"I never wear a hat," Eric grinned. "Grew up that way, down in Georgia—they almost had to lasso me to get shoes on me."

Traile laughed, but as they went out into the misty night his lean face quickly sobered. "Almost as bad as Limehouse—or the China Coast," he muttered, half to himself.

Eric shook his head in mock disgust. "I thought I'd been around, in my three years with World Radio and Cables—but compared with you I'm an old stay-at-home."

"There are some places I wish I'd never seen," Traile said with a sudden grimness. He started along the fog-choked sidewalk, moving with an oddly silent tread. Eric strode along beside him, his pipe crackling as mist particles touched the smoldering tobacco.

BETWEEN THE Occidental and a row of darkened shops was a narrow alley. They had crossed it, and were almost out of the blurred light from the restaurant, when a low hum of gears sounded near the curb. Traile looked around quickly. A long, black limousine was swinging away from where it had been parked. A curtain at the rear window had been partly raised.

He had a glimpse of a half-veiled face—a face of exotic beauty. The girl's red lips were parted as though to cry out something to them. But before she could speak, a yellow arm appeared. A huge hand was clasped over her lips, and she was hastily dragged back into the darkness of the car. The next moment the limousine had vanished in the murk.

Eric Gordon, with an angry shout, had started to dash after the black machine. Traile caught him, held him back. Eric turned on him furiously. "Let me go! Didn't you see? She's being kidnapped!"

"It's a trick," Traile said curtly. "Listen—they've stopped!"

From somewhere in the fog came a low, eerie whistle. Traile whirled as though he had been shot. "Quick—back to the restaurant!"

His sudden jerk at Eric's arm knocked the other man's pipe from his hand. As Eric lunged after it, there was a swift pat-pat of feet from the black entry of a shop. Traile spun, one hand lifted. In a tigerish leap, that crouching figure was on him, and the deadly noose was hissing down over his head.

But for his upraised hand, it would have been the end. With

a desperate sweep, he hurled the noose up and away from his head. Before the strangler could fling it back, he had the man's wrist in a viselike grip. A shrill cry burst from the strangler's lips, and almost on the instant two Chinese jumped from out of the fog. The first one sprang at Eric, a dagger raised for a murderous blow. Eric lashed out with an uppercut, and the yellow man stumbled backward.

As the two assassins appeared from the mists, Traile gave a terrific wrench at the strangler's arm. A bone cracked under that sudden jiu-jitsu twist, and with a groan the man dropped to the sidewalk. Just in time, Traile jumped aside, as the second Chinese plunged. A vicious jab to the ribs sent the killer back against the wall. He rebounded with a snarl, one hand clawing for Traile's throat.

But that clawing hand never came near its goal. With a lightning shift, the tall American struck. The clutching fingers writhed in empty air, and the Oriental wobbled to the ground from a thudding left to the jaw. Michael Traile wheeled to aid Eric, but the strangler came up with a rush. Broken arm dangling, he made one last attempt to hurl the silken noose. Traile side-stepped and struck all in one motion. Gasping, the other man fell. There was an ugly, crunching sound as his head struck a corner of the show-case window, then he lay still.

Eric Gordon had knocked the dagger from the hand of the first Chinese. The two men were locked in a fierce struggle, and as Traile leaped toward them the second Chinese scrambled to his feet and lunged to help the other. Then suddenly he saw Traile.

"Ai! Kai dai!" he screeched.

The other Chinese jumped back, and in a twinkling both of them disappeared in the fog. Traile waited tautly, his right hand curled around the butt of the gun he had drawn from under his coat. Gears clashed, and he heard the limousine speed away in the mist. He waited a second longer, turned to the half-dazed Gordon.

"Are you all right?" he asked in an undertone.

"I guess so," Eric said breathlessly. "But, good Lord, what's it all about?"

"Not so loud," warned Michael Traile, "I don't want any crowd here."

EXCITED VOICES were audible from beyond the Occidental. Traile drew Eric back into the dark shop-entry. Three men hurried by, peering around in the gloom. Traile waited until they had gone, then knelt beside the crumpled body of the strangler. As he dragged it out of the deeper shadow, the man's dark face was vaguely revealed in the dim light from the restaurant. Blood had trickled over his fierce-set-jaw, from a terrible gash in his head. The noose was still clenched in his hand.

"Is he dead?" whispered Eric, in an awed tone.

"Yes, unfortunately," was Traile's glum answer. "We might have made him talk—though I doubt it. His breed very seldom does."

"Then you know who he is?" exclaimed Eric.

"One of the deadliest species on earth," Traile responded, as he hurriedly unfastened the dead man's coat. "He was a Burmese thug—a professional strangler."

"I thought all of that stuff had been stamped out," said Eric, staring at the thug. "Anyway, what could have brought him clear over here?"

Traile did not answer. He had ripped the dead man's shirt away from his right shoulder, was bending down close to look at the bared flesh. Three Chinese characters were just discernible against the thug's dark skin.

"Odd," he said in a puzzled tone. "It must be a new symbol."

Eric Gordon leaned over and stared at the marks. "Branded! What can it all mean?"

"It means," Traile said in a queer, hard voice, "that he was a slave of the Invisible Emperor, Dr. Yen Sin—the most dangerous fiend who ever walked the earth!"

Eric looked at him blankly. "But I've never even heard of him."

"God help you if he should ever decide to change that," Traile said grimly. "This is the third attempt which has been made upon my life—because I learned too much of what he plans to do."

The younger man shook his head dazedly. "But this is the United States—things like that can't happen—"

"I suppose this was a dream," Traile said drily.

"It seems like one, all right," Eric now mumbled. He looked down at the thug and shivered. "It's incredible to think of his being sent clear across the Pacific to kill you."

"I didn't say that," replied Traile. He was swiftly searching the dead Burman's pockets. "He may have come here from New York—Chicago—or San Francisco. Yen Sin's headquarters are in China, but the Invisible Empire is spreading its long tentacles into every part of the globe. I've already warned—" he broke off, and a moment later the shielded rays of a small flashlight played on a lumpy area in the lining of the thug's coat.

He was starting to tear the cloth when a man and a woman emerged from the Occidental and came toward them. Traile instantly switched off the flashlight, but the woman had spied the grim tableau. With a scream, she turned and ran back to the door of the restaurant. Her escort followed, and in a moment their shouts for police echoed through the night.

Traile holstered his gun, stooped and lifted the dead man. Without apparent effort, he slung the body over his shoulder and hurried toward his car. Eric trotted at his side, looking back anxiously as a police whistle suddenly shrilled.

"Never mind him," said Traile coolly. "He can't see anything. Get out my keys—left coat pocket."

Another pedestrian glimpsed the limp form on Traile's shoulder just as they reached the sedan. He jumped back, raced into the fog, yelling at the top of his voice.

"Quick—take the wheel!" Traile rapped at Eric. "We don't want to explain to anyone just now."

He opened the rear door, dumped the body on the floor. Eric sent the sedan plunging into the mist at a reckless pace.

"Slow down," ordered Traile, as they skidded into Fifteenth Street. "If anyone followed us, we've shaken him."

HE CLIMBED over into the rear, was back in a few seconds

with an envelope which had been sewn into the strangler's coat lining. The outside bore no address, though there were dirty fingerprints on it as though it had passed through a number of hands. Traile took a pencil and carefully slit the envelope. Within were two small, folded sheets bearing words in a foreign language. One of them had been torn diagonally at the top, so that the first part was missing.

"Written in Ramasi—the old jargon of thuggee," he commented as he held the first sheet close to the dash-lamp.

"Don't tell me you can read that stuff?" said Eric, amazed.

"Not any too well—it's a corruption of Hindustani—but I'll try it." Traile now frowned over the words for a minute. "It seems to be a report from some surgeon in India, translated into Ramasi... *and the Hindu doctor evidently scraped or removed some vital portion of that lobe of the brain. At first, the effect was not noticed, for the operation seemed successful. Then it was noticed that the child did not sleep—*"

"Good Lord, Michael, what's the matter?" Eric Gordon gasped.

Traile's bronzed face, in the wan light of the dash-lamp, had suddenly turned gray under its tan. He stared at the paper as though some poisonous reptile had materialized in his hand.

"What's the matter?' Eric cried again.

"Nothing," said Traile, thickly. He hesitated, then went on in a leaden voice.

"It was then realized that the surgeon had destroyed the portion of the brain which enables the subconscious to take over the mind. All efforts to make the child sleep were in vain. Drugs were tried,

11

and found useless. The child grew thinner, and was expected to die. The parents, over the protests of the doctor, engaged a Yoga miracle man who claimed to be able to save its life. This he did, by the well known fakir trick of complete relaxation of the muscles. The child's attention was caught and held by a mechanical device, until the mind was completely withdrawn from all physical action. This was repeated until gradually it became a fixed habit. At the age of two and one half years, three months after the accident causing the operation, the boy was in perfect health.

"The parents then returned with him to America, but at the request of the hospital officials at Jubbulpore, confidential reports were sent as to the child's progress. American psychologists pointed out to the parents that the child must be educated on unique lines, and that a normal life of health depended on his keeping mentally occupied with new and fresh subjects, also that a proper balance likewise should be made in his physical life. A day tutor and a night tutor were engaged, along with a physical instructor as the child reached the age of five. By this time, because of his constant mental development, he was the equal of a normal child of eight or nine. When he was nine, he had the brain of a fourteen-year old and now thoroughly understood his own peculiar situation.

"From then on, he developed complete independence, making up his own schedule. As nearly as the reports to the hospital can indicate, he was even then quite accomplished in three or four languages, and adept at such sports as wrestling, boxing, and archery. The twelfth-year report shows that his brain was speeding up. He had learned to control his relaxation-periods perfectly, so that his muscles were completely relaxed even when he was engaged in serious reading or *thought. But at fifteen, a slump occurred. Apparently—though the report is vague—he realized desolation in being different from other boys. Particularly, he was failing to find happiness because he was advanced mentally so far beyond those of his age."*

Traile looked up, a strange, burning expression in his dark eyes. He glanced at Eric, but there was only a puzzled look on the younger man's face.

"He became morbid, and his parents suggested travel. For a time—from sixteen to twenty—this kept him busy. The reports are sketchy, but a partial list of the countries visited indicates he must almost have covered the world. Then the reports cease, in the year when his parents were killed in an accident—"

THE PAPER tore under Traile's taut fingers. He looked up, with a mirthless smile on his lips. "Well, Eric, do you understand now? Don't you *get* the gist?"

Eric stared at him with slowly increasing amazement.

"You mean—this boy was—*you?*"

A faint trace of the whimsical light came back into Michael Traile's eyes.

"As nearly as I can remember, Eric. You see, that was a long time ago—for a man who has never slept."

"Good Heavens," Eric burst out. "I should think you'd go mad!"

"That's the reason for my hobbies—my studies—my eternally keeping busy." The bitterness of Traile's words increased. "Be thankful, that you can lie down—close your eyes, and shut out the world for a few blessed hours. I have never known a single instant of forgetfulness—in twenty-seven years!"

Eric drew a long breath. "I can see it must be hell some-times—but think of all you've packed into those years. All you've seen and learned."

Traile stuffed the papers into his pocket, with a gesture of finality. "Let's forget it. We've a dead man on our hands, and the best way to avoid—" He stopped short, his eyes riveted on the envelope which had fallen to the floor.

Mist had seeped in through the window, settling upon the paper. And there on its surface, which had been blank, faint hieroglyphics were appearing. He snatched it up, his dark eyes racing over the characters.

"Good God!" he whispered. "Start the motor—drive to the Department of Justice as fast as you can!"

"What did that thing say?" Eric asked hastily, as he obeyed.

"It told me I've been a blind fool," Traile replied fiercely. "I should have guessed he was carrying this letter to no one else. Yen Sin—the Yellow Doctor—is here in Washington!"

CHAPTER 2
THE PIERCING DEATH

TRAILE WAS staring out into the blur-red white tunnels made by the headlights. His bronzed face had a grim look.

"What are you going to do—go after him with G-men?" Eric asked in a tense voice.

"No, I want to get this dacoit's body behind locked doors,

before Dr. Yen Sin hears what happened. I suspect that those three branded characters form a secret message."

The sedan ploughed through the fog with Eric hunched over the wheel, his empty pipe gripped between his teeth.

"Look here," he said eagerly, "why not get a dragnet out for that Chinese devil? With his gang of killers, he ought to be easy to spot."

"You don't know that yellow fiend," responded Traile. "He's made the name 'Invisible Emperor' mean just about that. His agents always precede him into an area where he intends to operate. They prepare a safe hiding-place, and when he moves he covers every step. I've heard that he alters his appearance when he travels, and almost invariably moves at night."

"But, confound it, he's still human," protested Eric.

A shadow crossed the taller man's lean face.

"Sometimes I wonder. Yen Sin is devoid of every human emotion, except hate and greed. I don't think I'm very easily affected, but the one look I had at his face is still like a nightmare. The man is Evil incarnate."

Traile had switched off the dash-light and drawn out his pistol from its armpit holster as he spoke. Eric glanced quickly across at him, then laughed a little shakily.

"Say, he *must* be bad—from the look on your face."

Traile's dark eyes, in the reflected glow from the lights, had taken on a flinty hardness.

"When you have come close to a horrible death," he said, "you remember the man who decreed it."

Eric's youthful face sobered.

15

"I swear, this business is enough to give a fellow the jitters."

"I should never have taken you up on that dinner invitation," Traile said moodily. "But I thought I had shaken them off when I reached San Francisco."

"I wouldn't have missed all this for a thousand bucks," retorted Eric. "I haven't had so much excitement since I socked a *gendarme* in Paris."

TRAILE SMILED in spite of himself. There was something infectious in Eric's irrepressible spirit. It was the first time in the latter half of his strange and lonely existence that he had felt such a strong and immediate bond of comradeship. A trifle sadly, he realized that he, too, but for a trick of Fate, might have been carefree and young at heart, like this easy-going Southerner.

"But I still don't get the hang of the Invisible Empire idea," said Eric, peering ahead into the mists. "What is it—some kind of secret society like the old Italian Black Hand?"

Traile's smile vanished abruptly.

"The Black Hand was a Sunday School picnic, compared with the Invisible Empire. It's an international league made up, oddly enough, of criminals and also their victims. On its rolls are murderers, criminals of every degree and a dozen nationalities, espionage agents Yen Sin has bribed or literally stolen from foreign powers—and finally his victims, the unwilling members caught in his web."

"I don't see how he could make anyone join, and be sure they wouldn't talk," objected Eric.

Traile laughed a trifle harshly.

"You'd learn—if he decided he needed you for some reason. If bribes don't work, he looks for a secret in the person's life—a basis for blackmail. Sometimes he frames up a case which makes the victim seem guilty when he or she is innocent. If nothing else works, he resorts to force. And once they're members of his Empire, there's only one way out. Death."

"That girl in the limousine!" exclaimed Eric. "Surely, she wasn't a criminal. She was trying to warn us—"

"I told you it was a trick," Traile

cut in shortly. "Her part was to decoy you away until the others finished me."

"But she looked so—" Eric hesitated.

"Beautiful, yes," Traile said dryly. "But don't confuse beauty with innocence. She is probably as deadly as the symbol of Dr. Yen Sin."

"What's that?" inquired the younger man.

"A cobra."

"I don't believe it," Eric said obstinately. He slowed the car, trying to glimpse a street-corner sign. "She looked frightened to death. That yellow rat who grabbed her has probably choked her to death."

"More likely," Traile replied a bit curtly, "she's desperately trying to make up for her failure, for that's one thing the Yellow Doctor seldom forgives."

"You mean he'd kill her?" Eric said, horrified.

"Perhaps, as an object lesson to the others, unless she is an important cog in his espionage machine."

Eric's face looked pale in the fog-reflected light.

"The damned butcher!" he said fiercely. "Why doesn't some-body bump him off—or at least turn him over to the police?"

"Men don't talk after they've seen a traitor put to the torture," Traile said with a sudden grimness. "There lies the secret of his power. He holds both agents and victims in sheer terror of his vengeance. No one knows when a spy of the Invisible Emperor may be at his elbow—or secretly watching."

Eric made the turn into Tenth Street, drove northward as fast as he dared.

"But what's it all going to get him?" he demanded. "What's he after?"

"Power!" said Traile, succinctly. "I'm personally convinced that he dreams of heading a yellow rebellion against the white race. I've tried to make the officials here see it, and they're at last waking up to the menace. Until Japan began slicing off China, he was well on the way to dominating Asia. Even the Soviet fears Yen Sin, and mentioning the Invisible Empire keeps the Japanese War Office awake at nights. It's hard to crush something that's invisible."

"But you said you'd seen him," interjected Eric. "You could identify him."

"Perhaps," Traile said ironically, "Dr. Yen Sin had the same idea when he sent out orders to have me removed."

Eric looked down for a second at the automatic in the other man's bronzed hand.

"So that's why you go armed," he muttered. "I'd forgotten—you said this was the third attempt."

"Right," Traile said. He motioned toward the windshield. "And that's why all the glass in this car is bullet-proof, also the windows in my apartment. My curiosity about the sensations of sleep doesn't extend to any permanent demonstration."

The young Southerner gave him a glance of sudden admiration.

"You certainly take it coolly. If I knew that yellow devil was after me, I'd light out for—"

"Slow down," Michael Traile interrupted crisply. "We're almost to the Court entrance."

Eric put on the brakes, and the sedan crawled along close to the curb. Traile swiftly lowered one window.

"Switch off the lights, and coast with the motor off for a second."

THE OTHER man complied in haste, tensing a little at the note in Traile's voice. Traile leaned out, but his keen ears detected no sound of another car. They had not been followed. In a moment the vague bulk of the huge, new Court Building loomed at the left. On their right, a street-light made a dim, fuzzy splotch of yellow in the fog.

"Drive in and switch on the dimmers," he told Eric. "The watchman will let us in."

The machine halted before the entrance to the dark courtyard, and the dimmed lights fell on a large ornamental, yet solid, iron gate which barred the way. In a few moments the watchman appeared. Traile leaned out and spoke hurriedly, and as the man recognized his voice he quickly unfastened the gate.

"Say, don't tell me you're a G-man," Eric exclaimed, as Traile motioned for him to drive in.

"No," Traile answered a bit tersely, "I just drop in now and then to see John Glover, head of the F.B.I."

The big gate was almost open, and Eric was starting to put the car in gear when Traile jerked around suddenly, gazing back toward the murky street. The next instant he had jumped to the ground, with a hasty command for Eric to drive inside. But the younger man followed him from the car.

"What's up?" he said anxiously.

Before Traile could reply, a slender figure appeared from the fog, the figure of the girl who had been in the limousine. She was breathing hard, as though she had been running, and through the silken half-veil, Traile could see that her dark eyes were dilated with some desperate emotion.

"Turn off the lights—drive inside the gate!" she gasped, and even in that tense moment he caught the strange, rich vibrancy of her voice.

He had partly towered the automatic, but his narrowed eyes did not leave her face.

"The Doctor works quickly," he said in a grim voice.

Her red lips twisted as though in violent pain.

"For God's sake, believe me! I have come to tell you something. I am risking my life…."

She had come so close that he could see the swift rise and fall of her breast. She was even more beautiful than that brief glimpse in the limousine had shown. Some delicate Oriental perfume added its haunting fragrance to her already exotic allure, and a different man than Michael Traile might readily have succumbed to the desperate appeal in her eyes. But he had known other agents of the Invisible Emperor, almost as lovely, and each as treacherous as a serpent.

"Where is the dacoit?" she whispered, and he felt the fingers on his arms tremble as she spoke. "You must get rid of his body. It means death for both of you unless—"

"So that's it," rapped Traile. He holstered the gun, wheeled to Eric, who was staring at the girl as though mesmerized. "Drive the car down into the basement. I'll be there in a minute."

He took the girl's arm in a firm grasp. Eric glared at him.

"Can't you see she's telling the truth? I knew I was right the other time—"

"Do as I told you!" There was a whiplash quality in Traile's suddenly altered tone. "If you don't value your own life, I value mine!"

ERIC'S FISTS clenched, but he turned to obey. He had not taken two steps when a queer, muffled *pat-a-pat* sounded from the mists. As he whirled, the girl gave a choked cry and sprang back, jerking her wrist free from Traile's grip.

"It's Li Cheng!" she moaned. "He's followed me!"

Traile shot his right hand under his coat. In the same instant, a huge Chinese with a villainous face and a close-shaved skull, leaped from the darkness. As he saw Traile and Gordon, and the watchman at the gate, he started to spring back into the fog, shouting a high-pitched cry in Cantonese dialect.

"No, no!" the girl screamed at him. "Not that!"

Swift as a rattler, the Chinese spun around, and an enormous hand flashed out toward her wrist. Traile snatched out his gun, but before he could fire, Eric Gordon had blocked his aim. With all the fury of a wildcat, the other man hurled himself upon the Oriental. His sudden onslaught sent the Chinese back a few feet. One yellow hand whipped back out of sight, reappeared with a knife, seemingly from nowhere.

The blade flashed down, but with an incredibly quick movement, the girl struck the killer's arm aside. Before he could strike again, Eric's fist smashed squarely into his jaw. Traile jumped forward to drill the Chinese. Then, abruptly, he whirled. Another automobile had plunged out of the fog, was stopping

An enormous hand flashed out toward her wrist.

at the curb. Two shadowy figures were leaping out, and a third was halfway out of the rear seat, with something in his arms.

Just in time, Traile threw himself side-wise, as he saw the first man. It was a Burmese hillman, and at his lips was a blow-gun!

There was an ominous hiss, and the poisoned dart shot past his head. With a baffled snarl, the hillman tried to snap another dart into the tube. Traile fired. The Burman gave a curious little leap, pitched down without a sound. Almost like an echo of Traile's shot came the crash of the watchman's pistol. The second man from the car stumbled, went to his knees. The watchman fired again, and the other collapsed in the shadows beyond the gate.

Above the roar of the last shot, Traile heard the girl cry out frantically. He spun about. Eric Gordon had Li Cheng's right arm gripped in one hand, was slugging madly at the yellow man's face. The Chinese had twisted halfway around toward the street, and he seemed to be trying wildly to escape.

Suddenly the girl whirled toward the gate, pulling at Eric's sleeve. The Chinese jerked away and dived into the gloom. Traile pumped two shots after him, was about to fire again when the girl raced toward him, literally dragging Eric with her.

"Run!" she cried. "Don't stop to ask...."

AN ODD, roaring sound broke in on her frenzied plea. Traile backed swiftly through the gate, the girl and Eric beside him. He was calling out to the watchman, who was not to be seen, when a blinding, greenish light appeared behind the sedan. Above the fierce roaring rose the scream of someone in mortal agony. Then the watchman tottered back into view. The blood froze in Traile's veins as he saw that staggering figure.

Green smoke was pouring from a spot in the watchman's back. With an icy horror, he realized that a hole had been burned clear through the man's body.

For only a fraction of a second, the ill-fated watchman swayed there on his feet. Like a puppet suddenly released, he sagged to the ground. A little beyond, the dead Burman was visible in the terrific glare, but everything else was hidden back of the light.

Traile had thrown one hand before his eyes, to shield them from the heat and light. Without moving it, he raised his other hand and emptied his gun into the center of the green inferno. The dazzling light danced crazily, and he thought he heard a shriek through the constant, dull roar which accompanied the glare. He backed farther away, saw Eric shielding the girl, both of their faces starkly outlined in the emerald light.

As abruptly as it had appeared, the green light vanished. There was a second when opaque, green smoke hid the entire scene, and in that moment Traile could hear running feet—the low, familiar *pat-pat* of an Oriental. Then the engine of the other car speeded up, and with a rasp of gears it raced away in the night.

Michael Traile slowly turned. The girl shrank under his gaze, put out one hand in a pitiful gesture.

"I didn't know!" she whispered. "Please—please believe me."

Traile's lean, tanned face was like granite.

"Keep hold of her, Eric," he said coldly, and turned toward the sedan. But she stopped him with an exclamation.

"Wait—you don't know what may be hidden there."

He halted, his eyes for the first time holding a trace of doubt. He took a step toward her.

"If you're sincere, then why were you in on that murder plot tonight?"

The half-veil had been thrown back, and he could clearly see the look of despair on her face.

"I was tricked. I did not know—"

His dark eyes searched the even darker, almost black depths of hers, while Eric stood hostilely watching him.

"You're lying," he said calmly. "Yen Sin holds you in his power. You were obeying his orders to trap me."

A shudder ran over her slender form at mention of the Invisible Emperor. Eric caught her as she swayed against him. She shook her head, looked up at him from under her curling black lashes. Her brief smile held a world of pathos.

"Thank you, but I am all right," she said in a low, hopeless voice. She straightened, and then—in the moment when he had relaxed his hold—sprang to the other side of the car and was lost in the mist before Traile could head her off.

A slow flush came into Eric's face as he met Traile's ironic glance.

"Lesson Number One," Traile said acidly.

"But—but I still can't believe she's a murderess," Erie mumbled. "She honestly tried to save us just now."

"So that they could finish their work," retorted Traile. "Come on, we'll see if I'm right."

He went around the side of the sedan. The rear door was open, and lying half out of the car was the body of the thug. His coat and shirt, which Traile had partly replaced, had been cut away with a sharp knife. And where the three characters had been was now only a gruesome patch of raw flesh. The other man had been carried off.

"Holy smoke!" said Eric hoarsely. "They cut it right off him!"

"In their hurry, they missed part of the first character. Almost half of it is still here, but I'm afraid it won't help us any."

Eric dazedly moved his head.

"It's too much for me. How did they know we were here, and what was that devilish green light?"

Traile had shoved the dacoit's body into the car and closed the door.

"I don't know," he said soberly, "but I do know the fiend who contrived it."

He knelt by the dead watchman, while Eric gazed on with an awed expression. The look of agony on the dead man's face was indescribable. Traile steeled himself and lifted the limp body from the ground. For an instant, he met Eric's sickened eyes across the inert form. Then they both stared down, in grim fascination, at the horrible, bloodless hole which showed in the watchman's breast.

CHAPTER 3
THE INVISIBLE EMPEROR

I N AN almost soundless room, somewhere in Washington, a blindfolded man stood tensely, fearfully waiting. He stood alone, a solid, middle-aged figure in white Navy uniform, with the three gold stripes of a commander on his shoulder-straps. But for the desperation on his florid face, and the blindfold which covered his eyes, he would have been an authoritative figure, and even now there was a certain fierce dignity about him in spite of his helpless pose.

He stood, listening intently, the twitching of his hands betraying his wire-tight nerves. He had not yet seen the room, for he had been fed to it blindfolded, but it seemed to be alive with a kind of hushed menace. A vague earthy smell was perceptible, though almost obscured by another odor, sickeningly sweet. At first, the second odor seemed to be incense, but after a moment he knew it for the reek of opium.

For five minutes he waited, with perspiration rolling down his face from the blindfold, for the room was damply warm. The only sound came from somewhere above him, a low, monotonous rustling which was close to being a hiss. Then suddenly he gave a violent start, for a sibilant voice was speaking.

"You may remove the blindfold, Commander Lee."

With shaking hands, the naval officer pulled the cloth from his eyes. He stared around blankly, for there was no one to be seen. He stood in the center of the strangest room he had ever known. There were no windows, nor any sign of the way through which he had been brought. An exquisite Persian tapestry covered the wall at his right, and a companion piece hung from rings high up on the left wall. In front of him, and less clearly seen, was a black wall ornamented with red and gold figurines engaged in various dances. Three sets of Chinese gongs hung from the ceiling, colored tassels dangling.

The only light came from a huge brass dragon lamp fastened to the ceiling. The thing had been carved by a master, for even without the pale green light which it seemed to breathe from its nostrils, and which streamed from its glaring eyes, it had a startling malevolence. From where the commander stood, it appeared to be glaring straight down at him, and as he gazed up he realized that this dragon lamp was the source of the low, ominous rustling. Evidently the sound came from the gas which provided the light.

After that single command to him, the sibilant voice had remained silent. He looked around furtively. The wall behind him was hidden by two duplicate Indian prints. There was, to his surprise, no rug on the floor. The barren stone, cracked and darkened with age was in ugly contrast to the rich Oriental color of the room.

Another minute passed, then to the officer's straining ears came a faint, almost imperceptible sliding sound. He peered into the darker side of the room. The dragon lamp had been placed so that its pallid light shone away from that side, making it difficult to see. Apparently there had been no change. The black wall seemed the same—but no, there had been, on that instant, a faint quivering of the dancing figures!

With a quick-
ening of pulses, he
knew what had
happened. The
wall was com-
posed of two
sliding sections
which rolled back
into niches at the
sides. Just behind
was a painted
black curtain,
made to resemble

the wall and to hide the rest of the room. He had no time for
more than a swift glance, for the voice he had learned to dread
was speaking again.

"And now, Commander, your report, if you please."

The silky, mocking voice of the hidden speaker was like a
dagger sheathed in velvet. Commander Lee's florid face turned
gray-white.

"I—I haven't been able to learn all you wanted," he said
hoarsely. "I got the plans for the new submarines, but the
other—" His words faded away helplessly.

There was a long silence, followed by a sharp tapping, as of
pointed fingernails against some hard surface. The sound came
from behind the curtain.

"The submarine plans are unimportant—now," said the unseen
man. The words were English, with a slight guttural accent, but

so slight as to be hardly noticeable. "You were instructed to bring full details of this new 'Q-Group' which is designed to wreck the Invisible Empire. I am waiting."

Lee made a helpless gesture.

"I've already told you all I know. There are five men in the group. One to operate with the White House secret service, one with the State Department, the others with the War, Navy, and Justice Departments. I tried to find out from the Chief of Naval Intelligence just who they are, but he froze up. He wouldn't even admit there was such a group."

"And what of the man called Michael Traile?" asked the hidden speaker

softly. "Is he one of the group?"

"I tell you I don't know—I can't find out," the naval officer said desperately. "I saw him in the Bureau once, and that's all I know!"

"Defiance, Commander?" There was a sudden hardness in that silken voice.

"No—no! But—Oh, God, why can't you let me go? I've paid a hundred times over for what I did in Shanghai. You've made me betray my country—sell my soul...."

"Enough!"

The word crackled from behind the curtain, and the menace of it cut off Lee's torrent of words as though a floodgate had closed.

"You will return to your duties," the hidden man directed icily, after a pause. "Tomorrow you will contrive to get the Chief of Naval Intelligence to a certain lonely spot I shall suggest. My men will then take over the situation."

"No!" The rising tide of the officer's desperation suddenly burst all its bounds. "No, damn you! I won't do it! By God, I'll kill you before I...."

His voice rose to a scream and broke. He thrust one hand under his white uniform blouse, snatched out a gun, and leaped toward the painted curtain. With a furious gesture, he swept it aside and raised the pistol. But that hastily lifted arm stiffened even as he aimed it, and, trembling, he stood there like a man in a dream, his finger lax on the trigger.

Like a living picture of Satan, a yellow face looked out at him. He had a dazed glimpse of the Crime Lord's terrible smile—of that hideous face like a mask against the teakwood chair. Then everything vanished, save the awful eyes of Dr. Yen Sin.

PARALYZED, AND helpless, Lee stood there, gazing into their depths. For a moment, the pupils contracted, till they were but deadly black points. Then, as the tawny yellow of Yen Sin's eyes was revealed, it seemed as though a tiger looked out through that saffron, pointed face. A second longer, that color remained, flecked with green as bright as an emerald. Then, swiftly, the pupils enlarged again, growing until they were like black pools—horrible, malignant.

The naval officer took a faltering step forward, the gun sinking to his side. He had a terrible sense of being drawn into those sinister black pools... of being sucked into some bottomless pit....

"You will lay down your pistol—here," that evil voice came as from a great distance.

Obediently Lee placed the weapon on the right arm of the great teakwood chair. Dr. Yen Sin touched it with the closed fan in his right hand, while the long yellow fingers of his left toyed with an oval box on the other chair-arm. He smiled, glanced at something across the naval officer's shoulder.

"Perhaps, Commander, you would like to see the fate from which I saved you."

The officer drew himself up. The black pools had receded. He could see again the rest of that mocking, satanic face, with its black and slanting eyebrows, and the mandarin mustache....

Slowly, he looked around. A section of tapestry had been drawn aside, and standing there, stripped to the waist, was a Hindu with a jeweled knife. His fierce eyes met the commander's with an angry, baffled look. Dr. Yen Sin spoke a few words in a tongue which the officer did not understand. The Hindu vanished, and the panel silently closed. The strange, malignant eyes of the Crime Emperor returned to Lee.

33

"I am afraid you have made an enemy, Commander. Ram Ghar feels that you cheated him because you failed to carry through your plan."

Great beads of perspiration stood out on Lee's brow.

"What are you going to do with me?" he whispered.

Dr. Yen Sin smiled.

"You refer to your forcibly making my personal acquaintance? Or to the attempt at—murder?"

The officer cringed, for the eyes of the Yellow Doctor had taken on a queer light, totally at variance with his thin smile.

"It was very—unwise," Yen Sin went on, suavely. "Have you forgotten what happened to Lieutenant Broward, at Manila?"

A look of horror distorted the naval officer's face. Dr. Yen Sin raised the ebony fan and tapped twice on the arm of the chair.

"For God's sake, not the torture!" groaned the commander.

The mockery of a smile on that satanic face deepened.

"You are unduly alarmed, Commander." Yen Sin sat back against the carved chair, gently moving the now opened fan. "Surely you would not have me forget my duty to a guest?"

Slippered feet made a faint sound in the darkness as he spoke. A pretty little Chinese girl appeared, attired in native costume, shuffling along in her tiny sandals like an automaton. In her hands she held a silver tray on which were two small glass goblets and a silver pitcher, engraved in the Italian fashion of at least a century past. Her face was turned so that she would not be looking at the robed figure in the chair. Just for an instant, her almond eyes flicked toward the naval officer. A queer expression swept into them, then she hastily knelt in the shadow which covered that end of the room.

The Crime Emperor removed the goblets and the pitcher, motioned for the girl to withdraw with the tray. The commander was looking in terror at the pitcher of wine. Yen Sin laid down the fan.

"Set your fears at rest, Commander Lee. I shall drink with you. And you may inspect the goblets, if you desire."

HE PAUSED, as though listening to something, and Lee saw him turn his head to one side. The yellow hand which had stretched toward the pitcher suddenly clenched so that the sharp nails dug into Yen Sin's flesh. All the mocking expression disappeared from his face in a twinkling, leaving it so utterly ferocious that the naval officer backed away in renewed panic. Then to Lee's amazement, the Yellow Doctor spoke swiftly in Chinese, his head still turned aside, though there was no one else in the room. When he had finished, he turned back, and as by magic the suavely courteous mask descended upon his face.

"A trifling interruption; I am very sorry."

Lee had watched him intently and he continued to do so as the doctor filled the two goblets, but at no time was Yen Sin's hand near either glass. The Yellow Doctor lifted one goblet, touched it against the embroidered symbol on his mandarin robe, then to Lee's glass.

"To the house of Yen Sin—and your health, Commander."

The officer raised his glass in an unsteady hand. His face was deathly pale, but as Yen Sin drained his glass some of the color came back into Lee's pasty cheeks. He drank one cautious sip, then slowly emptied the goblet.

"And now," said the Crime Emperor, with a subtle change of tone, "there is but one detail before you resume your honorable station as an American officer. Describe this Michael Traile."

"Then—then I am to go free?" the other man gasped, in relief.

"At once," nodded the Yellow Doctor. His tawny eyes were fixed on Lee's face. "And now, this description?"

"He's tall, at least six feet, deeply sunburned, and he has dark eyes and almost black hair." The commander thought for a moment. "His face is a bit inclined toward being thin. He's usually carefully dressed. I think he has a comfortable private income."

Yen Sin's eyes had narrowed, accentuating the satanic outlines of his yellow face.

"There is some mystery about this man Traile," he said sharply. "Something connected with his past—also his private life. Do you know anything about that?"

Lee shook his head.

"I tried to become friendly with him, as you—as you suggested. He politely rebuffed me. But I found out one thing. There is hardly any subject under the sun he doesn't know something about, in spite of his youth—"

He broke off, for a murderous flame had blazed up in Yen Sin's eyes. Then the Crime Emperor regained his cold self-control, and stood up. The silken yellow mandarin robe fell into long folds as he drew himself up to his full height. He stared down at the naval officer, and for the second time that night Lee had that evil sensation of being drawn into black and bottomless pools.

He shook himself, trying to fight off the feeling. Then he realized that Yen Sin was motioning him toward the other side of the room. His mind for an instant had seemed to stand still.... He had a sudden, uneasy feeling that there had been more than an instant—that perhaps minutes had passed while he stood there....

Then a stolid, pock-marked Chinese in civilian clothes appeared at the opened panel, a blindfold in his hand. Just before Lee's eyes were covered, he stole a glance back into the room. The painted curtain had fallen back into place. The low hissing of the green-eyed dragon was the only sound. But he had an odd, sinister feeling that the eyes of Dr. Yen Sin were on him as he was led away.

CHAPTER 4
THE DRAGON'S SHADOW

WITHIN THE modern gray-and-chromium office of Director Glover, Chief of the Federal Bureau of Investigation, a brief silence had fallen. At last Glover leaned back in his leather chair, the light of his desk-lamp glinting on the prematurely silver hair at his temples.

"Understand, Wiggam, Traile's name is not to appear in any records or even in coded correspondence and messages. These secret orders to our district and foreign agents will mention him solely as Q-5. He will identify himself by his right in-dex-finger, a copy of which will be sent at once to all stations, with instructions to cooperate with him implicitly."

Wiggam, the thin little assistant director, pursed his lips disapprovingly. "Too much power for any one agent, I'd say."

"For the third time," snapped Glover, "I tell you Traile is no ordinary agent. He's a free-lance, and D.J. is only one of the departments he works with."

"And you say there are five of these Q-Men?" Wiggam sniffed.

Glover hesitated, his deep-set gray eyes resting on the State Department letter before him.

"I guess you'd better know the truth, in case he contacts the Bureau when I'm not here. Officially, the Q-Group consists of five men picked to combat this mysterious Chinese doctor. The State Department has let it leak out that there is such a unit, and that it's composed of five men who know the face of Dr. Yen Sin. The rumor is that they are agents who have purpose-ly let themselves be forced into the Invisible Empire. Actually, four of them are non-existent."

"Eh?" said Wiggam, startled.

"Michael Traile is the entire Q-Group," Glover explained bluntly. "The State Department hit on this idea to protect him, since he is the only one who knows much about Yen Sin—except his victims and agents. This way, the doctor will be searching for five secret agents instead of concentrating on one, even if he suspects Traile is one of the five. The scheme is carried out by using a different number for each department where he's been given special authority. Q-1 covers him when he's acting with the White House secret service; the State Department lists him as Q-2; he's Q-3 with the War Department, Q-4 for Navy, and with us, Q-5. The idea can be extended to any other government unit. And he has a designated contact officer in each department or bureau."

Wiggam looked down his thin little nose. "Very peculiar, that we couldn't handle this 'Invisible Emperor' our own way. We have three agents who speak Chinese."

"We *had* three," Glover said grimly. "They've vanished."

Wiggam's pinched lips opened in dismay, but there came a sudden interruption. Glover's private door burst open, and a member of the local F.B.I. squad poked his head inside.

"Pardon me, Chief—but something queer's happened down in the court!"

Glover hurried across the hall into another office. A strange greenish light was fading out below.

"I heard shots, then this thing—" began the agent.

"Get five or six men down there," clipped Glover. He strode toward the nearest elevator, Wiggam trotting behind him. There was a brief delay, before the cage came up. A few moments later they emerged in the basement and ran through the underground garage of the Justice Building. As they started up the ramp, dim lights shone down it, and a sedan came to a stop.

"Michael!" exclaimed Glover, as he recognized the tall bronzed man who jumped from the running-board. "What the devil?"

"We'd better get inside, John," Traile said in a calm voice. "That gate's unguarded—and anything may happen."

Glover motioned to Wiggam. "Notify the guard's office."

G-MEN AND watchmen soon appeared. Glover sent them out to the entrance. Eric Gordon let the sedan roll down into the basement, and the director followed with Traile. As the car stopped, Traile opened the rear door. Glover looked in consternation at the two bodies within.

"A calling-card from Dr. Yen Sin," Traile said grimly. He pointed to the dead watchman. The man's clothing had been burned away in a circle, leaving his scorched and blackened chest completely bare. In the center was a hole about two inches in diameter, with the flesh at the edge burned to a crisp.

"My God!" Glover said quickly. "What horrible thing did this?"

"Some kind of chemical fire," Traile muttered. His lean face had a sick color in spite of its heavy tan. "The flame obviously cauterizes the blood vessels as it burns through."

Eric Gordon stood by; watching white-faced as Traile more closely examined the gruesome wound. Traile straightened, glanced for a second at the dead man's agonized face.

"Poor devil," he said under his breath. He beckoned to a staring garage attendant, and the body was quickly covered with a robe. Glover's first look of nausea had slowly changed into a fierce determination.

"Are you sure that Yen Sin was connected with this?" he demanded.

"Positive." Traile's dark eyes took on a smoldering fire as he described the events which had begun near the Occidental. Glover's square jaw set like a rock.

"This means a war to the finish! I'll have fifty undercover men here by morning. We'll comb the town."

"I'm afraid the Yellow Doctor is already too well hidden," Traile said moodily. "Tonight's action proves the Invisible Empire is fully organized here."

"But surely we can pick up a lead some way," protested Glover. "There's Chinatown—"

"Dr. Yen Sin has all the tongs completely cowed," interrupted Traile. "You could arrest every Chinese in Washington, and you wouldn't learn a thing. But there's one slim chance."

"What's that?" said Glover quickly.

Traile turned to Eric. "Think your stomach can stand a little more?"

"I guess so," said Erie. "What do you want?"

"Help me with the dacoit. It's just a minor operation before he goes to the morgue."

The body of the thug was stretched on a bench, face downward. Traile took a knife and, calmly as a surgeon, removed the piece of skin which bore the remainder of the Chinese letter. He held it up to the light.

"It wasn't branded—it was put on with some kind of solution."

"I'll take your word for it," Eric said, with a grimace.

"What are you going to do with that thing?" demanded Glover, as Traile wrapped it up in heavy paper.

"Compare it with some Chinese codes at my apartment." Traile turned toward his car, swung back. "Eric, you'd recognize that girl if you saw her again, wouldn't you?"

A dull red crept into the Southerner's face. "You needn't rub it in," he growled.

"Didn't mean it like that, old man." Traile glanced at Glover. "It might be a good idea to have Eric look over those photos and sketches of known spies. She looked like a foreign agent— the kind that Dr. Yen Sin recruits for the Empire."

He swept the curtain aside and raise the pistol.

"See here," Eric protested, "I'm not in the habit of making war on women."

The steel came back into Traile's voice. "Chivalry is all right, in its place. But the women who obey Yen Sin are as deadly as any of his killers."

"I still think—" Eric began obstinately, but the sentence was cut off by the arrival of Wiggam. The assistant director was plainly excited.

"Another queer message just came in on the teletype!" he exclaimed. "But this one's in some foreign language."

"You'd better come up, Michael," Glover said hurriedly. "Our interpreter isn't here at night."

The four of them quickly went to the elevator.

"The message just came in—it was on the Baltimore circuit," gabbled Wiggam. "But when Communications checked back, they said they never sent it."

"And that other one was on the New York circuit," Glover frowned. "Gordon, it looks as though you've another job on your hands."

Eric's blue eyes held a puzzled expression. "Even if the lines are tapped by induction, as Michael suggested, I can't see how anybody would know the right wires. The D.J. lines are only a few of the hundreds of telegraph wires between here and Manhattan."

THE ELEVATOR stopped at the fifth floor, and they hastened to the Communications section. In a moment, Traile was scanning the tape which held the mysterious message. Suddenly his dark eyes narrowed.

"What is it?" asked Glover anxiously. "Can you make it out?"

"It's written in Yunnan dialect, as the English Romanize it," said Traile. An ironic smile twisted his lips. "Quite considerate of him."

"Who?" demanded both Glover and Eric, in one breath.

"Our friend, the Yellow Doctor. This message is addressed to me. It reads: 'The hand of Fate is invisible.'"

"But what's the idea?" said Eric.

"It's a threat," Traile said grimly. "He's already learned what happened. But there's something odd about this. He never bothered with a warning before."

One of the teletype operators bent over the machine before him. "That line's gone dead again, sir," he said to Glover, "just the way it did before the message came."

Traile and the others gathered around the machine, watching the tape. Several minutes passed, and still it was blank. A curious look abruptly came into Traile's dark face.

"I've a sudden feeling this is a trick to keep us here," he said.

"For what reason?" snapped the director.

"I wish I knew." Traile lit a cigarette, inhaled thoughtfully. "It's one of two things—either something that will happen here, or to keep us away from some other place where he's planning a stunt."

Glover's solid jaw bulged. "I'd like to see that devil try anything around here!"

"It wouldn't be anything obvious." Traile took a few restless steps back and forth. "I think I'll go ahead. You can call me on our private wire if anything develops."

Eric and the director followed him into the hall. He was about to ring for one of the central elevators when a figure appeared from the hall that led to the Pennsylvania Avenue side of the building. Most of the hall lights had been put out, but the white uniform of a naval officer was distinguishable.

All three men had turned, for the Navy man was reeling along drunkenly. Traile peered into the dim-lit corridor.

"It's Commander Lee—one of the White House aides," he said *soto voce*. "Looks as though he's gone on a bender—"

He broke off, staring, as the naval officer came into the brighter light. Lee's face was a deep, ugly yellow, and his tongue was protruding like that of a man dying from thirst. His breath came in hoarse gasps.

"What's the matter, man?" Glover cried out in a shocked voice.

Lee's gaze twitched toward the three men. For a moment he stood there, swaying. His swollen lips were drawn back, and his eyes had a queer, pulled look. They narrowed, changed weirdly

even as his face was changing, taking on a startling likeness
to—

"Good God!" whispered Traile. "*The Dragon's Shadow!*"

For suddenly, that awful metamorphosis was complete. Gone
was the face of the Navy man. There before them was the yellow
visage of a Chinese, his lips drawn back in a hideous smile.
Traile's glance shot to the stricken man's hands. They, too, had
yellowed, and in their stiffened, claw-like appearance he recalled
another pair of hands—

"Look out, Eric!" he said swiftly. "Don't let him touch you!"

But that terrible figure in white made no attempt to seize
the closer man. With a hoarse, unintelligible cry, he sprang at
Traile, his hands outstretched like talons. Traile threw himself
backward. One yellowed claw caught his sleeve, and the cloth
tore with a savage rip. His backward jerk caused him to trip
over the mat by the elevator shaft. Before he could catch himself,
he fell to his knees.

A LOOK of ghoulish triumph came into the yellow face above
him. The officer flung himself down, his fingers stiffly spread.
They were almost at Traile's throat when Eric Gordon dived
in, with fists flailing. The commander gave a fierce grunt, like
an animal, and whirled on the younger man. Eric drove in a
short but furious jab to Lee's solar plexus. The naval officer
reeled back, doubled over. Glover had sprung forward to help
Eric, but his aid was not needed. With a gasping moan, Lee
crumpled to the floor.

Traile had regained his feet. As he bent over the fallen man,
Lee's tortured eyes fixed themselves on his face. His yellowed

hands reached up feebly. The white-clad officer made one last attempt to get to his feet, then a sudden trembling took hold of him. The clawing hands dropped back at his sides, and in another moment his harsh breathing ceased. Glover knelt beside him, looked up at Traile.

"Dead!" he said in an awed tone.

Traile slowly nodded. "The Dragon's Shadow always means death."

Eric shuddered. "What is it—some kind of disease?"

"I don't know. I've seen only one other case, though I'd heard stories of it in Shantung Province. An Englishman at Chefoo was found dead just like this. When rigor mortis set in you could hardly tell he was not Chinese."

"But the post-mortem?" Glover asked huskily. "Didn't it show the cause?"

"Nobody would touch him," Traile replied. "There was a rumor that a surgeon who had done a post-mortem in a similar case had died the same way."

"Judas Priest!" said Eric. "You don't think I could've caught it when I socked him, do you?"

"No, I think the surgeon must have died from an infection after cutting into the body. When I shouted that warning not to let him touch you, I was afraid he'd get his hands locked in your throat. The Englishman at Chefoo almost killed a man that way just before he died."

Glover stared down at Lee's yellowed face. "The Dragon's Shadow—why do they call it that?"

Traile shook his head. "I tried to find out, but even educated

Chinese seem in deathly fear of the subject. Only one man would even speak of it, and he warned me to forget I had ever heard of it."

Glover's eyes jerked up from the corpse. "I'd forgotten Yen Sin for a minute. He must be back of this devilish thing!"

"No doubt of it," Traile agreed somberly. "Even in Shantung, I had a suspicion that the Dragon's Shadow was in some way connected with the Invisible Empire."

"But how could a man like this—a Navy commander—a White House aide—be linked with Yen Sin?" demanded the director.

Traile's lean face shadowed. "Blackmail, probably. Yen Sin is an adept at finding the dark spots in any one's life."

"That teletype message!" said Eric. "You were right—it was meant to keep you here until this man came."

"I'm afraid that's the answer," Traile admitted, with a grim look at the dead commander. "He was sent here on a murder mission—but I doubt if he knew what he was doing."

"This is going to make a hell of a scandal," said Glover.

"It'll have to be hushed up," Traile responded quickly. "Don't report the death until I've called Mattison, at the State Department. He'll handle the press."

Glover rubbed his heavy jaw. "Maybe we ought to search Lee's quarters. There might be some clue to Yen Sin's hide-out, or some dope on the Invisible Empire."

"Not likely, but we can try it," Traile said crisply. "Know the address?"

"I'll get it."

Glover disappeared, came back almost at once. With him was a man to guard the dead man's body. Traile had summoned an elevator, and he and Eric were waiting in the cage. When they reached the basement garage, the morgue truck was just coming down the ramp. It swung alongside Traile's sedan, and the driver languidly climbed down.

"Two of 'em, huh?" he said, looking from the covered body of the watchman to the dark figure on the bench. Then he stared hard at the thug. "Say, that's funny—we already got a bird like that on ice."

Traile wheeled. "With his shoulder scraped, you mean?"

"No, there's some Chink tattooin' right about where this guy's been cut. But they're both the same size an' color—"

"How did the other man die?" rapped Traile.

"Drowned," said the morgue man, laconically. "Harbor cops fished him outa th' Channel, just before sun-down. Been in th' water a day or so."

"Will we need any order, to see him?" Traile asked swiftly.

"No, just tell Pete ya want to see him. There ain't no red tape down there."

A MINUTE later, Traile's sedan was again ploughing the fog. He was at the wheel, and Eric and Glover were crowded into the front seat with him, both having rejected the charred and bloodstained rear.

"What do you think it means?" Glover asked eagerly.

Michael Traile gazed thoughtfully into the mist. "It upsets my first idea. If the man were carrying part of a code message, too important even to trust to paper, Yen Sin wouldn't dispose of him like this even after he had read the code."

"Maybe he drowned accidentally," hazarded the F.B.I. director. "Dr. Yen Sin may not know about it."

"Quite possible. At any rate, I want to see those characters. If we could get a line on Yen Sin's purpose here in Washington, we'd be a long way toward blocking him."

There was an interval of silence, until the sedan swung into the heavily fogged stretches of Water Street. Eric sniffed the unsavory odors near one end of the market area.

"I'll think twice before inviting you to dinner again," he growled. "You pay me back with a double dose of murder and then—this blamed joy-ride to the morgue."

"You're lucky you're not taking the ride in the black wagon," Traile jested, but there was a faint grimness under his humor.

"I'll probably dream about murders," Eric complained with a note of mock grievance. "Say, there's one thing you've got the edge on the rest of us—you don't have any—" he stopped short, fumbling for words to cover the break.

"It's all right," Traile said wearily. "John happens to know of my—affliction."

"Hanged if I'd call it an affliction," said Glover emphatically. "I've been years trying to figure how to run on less sleep. If I could get as much out of life as you do—"

"I think we're almost there," Traile interrupted with a trace of curtness. His nerves were getting a little taut, the inevitable reaction of his peculiar physical make-up. He had made no attempt to relax his body after the swift action of the past hour.

One of the coffin lids was lifting.

It was his Achilles heel—the imperative need for recharging of his vitality by frequent rest-periods. Prolonged action without any relaxation-periods would bring on a state of exhaustion almost terrifying in its sudden effect. He had experienced it once, and had guarded against it thereafter.

Glover and Eric were silent as he switched on the spotlight and began to search through the mists. He edged in close to the curb as the car passed Seventh Street. The spotlight moved over the harbor police station, through the blur of fog to the old waterfront church which was now the morgue. He parked at an angle, the spotlight resting on a dirty stained-glass window at one side.

"Pretty little place," Eric commented drily as they started inside.

There was no one in the dingy little office. Traile looked around, called back through the inquest-room. There was no answer. He stared at the others, for the silence was suddenly ominous. As one, all three started back toward the rear of the building. They passed through the inquest-room, Traile a little ahead of the rest.

As he reached the door of the main rear room, he took a swift glance around. Then he halted, gazing in amazement at the grisly scene before him.

Lying flat on his back, a terrified light in his dead, glassy eyes, was the wizened figure of the morgue attendant. And there beside him, one dark hand almost on the other man's throat, was the corpse of the second Burman!

CHAPTER 5
THE INVISIBLE EMPEROR

THOUGH IT was only a second, every detail registered with photographic clearness on Traile's brain. The corpse of the thug lay sprawled as though it had leaped from the slab on which it had lain. Beyond the two bodies, several cheap potter's-field coffins were piled up erratically, by the door to the tiny room opening on the river. Light from a single electric bulb suspended from the ceiling, threw a pallid glow over the dead men, and the vaults where the bodies were kept. There was no living person in sight.

"Lord!" Glover said hoarsely as he glimpsed the two bodies. "That brown devil must have been alive—"

"The code!" Traile cut in sharply. "Look—it's gone!"

Glover and Eric bent over, following his pointed finger.

"It's been taken off with some kind of acid!" exclaimed Eric. "It must have been done in the last few minutes, too."

Out in the night, there sounded a deep, hoarse roar from the siren of a boat in the fog. It had barely died away when another blast sounded—from in front of the morgue—the quick, short response of an exhaust horn. Traile spun around. He was halfway to the inquest-room door when he caught something from the corner of his eye. He whirled back, then an icy shiver ran up his spine.

One of the coffin lids was lifting. With a sudden jerk, it opened wide, and a dark, vicious face appeared. A blow-gun flashed up to the killer's thick lips, the end aimed straight at

53

Glover. Traile's hand was at the V of his coat, but there was no time to draw his gun. With a shout to the F.B.I. chief, he hurled himself toward the coffin.

The crash of the lid and the hiss of the blow-gun seemed to come almost together. A wild yell broke from the lips of the Burman as Traile crushed the lid down upon him. Eric Gordon leaped and wrested the blow-gun from the man's half-protruding hand. Traile twisted around, looked anxiously at Glover.

"I'm O.K.," the director said tensely. "But look—out there on the river!"

The hull of a small black boat had loomed out of the fog. A yellow, evil face showed in the light from the morgue, the face of a Chinese with something shining in one raised hand….

"Run!" shouted Traile. He snatched at the drop-light, tore it loose from the ceiling. In the abrupt darkness, a shrill howling sound came from out of the night. Across at the harbor police station, a booming voice made a hasty, excited query.

Traile had shoved Eric toward the side door which led to the morgue-garage platform. He heard Glover pound through the inquest-room, then above the rattle of upset coffins as the Burman scrambled free came a dull, soft *plop*.

A muffled scream rose out of the darkness—the scream of a man in the throes of some horrible death. With his hand at his mouth and nostrils, Traile plunged through the side doorway and forward to the street. Above the screech of the dying native, he caught a faint hissing. The sound was lost in a crash of gunfire near the front of the building.

He ran down the incline to the platform, trying to see through the mists. A blurred form passed between the morgue and the sedan. He recognized the slinking gait of an Oriental. Red flame jetted from a spot nearby, and the Chinese pitched down with a wailing cry. Lights flashed up in the harbor police station.

Several bluecoats charged out into the fog as Traile reached the front of the morgue. He heard Glover shout something at the first man, then the roar of an engine drowned the rest. He sprang to the sedan, jerked the spotlight around. The beam flashed over a car, half hidden in the mist, then shone on a second machine which was swinging to follow the first.

But for the fog-blurred crest on its side, he would have thought it was the same limousine which had been parked near the Occidental. As it lurched ahead, the misty light fell on a figure in the yellow robes of a mandarin. For a flitting instant, a malignant face showed there in the glow.

Traile went rigid. The man in the limousine was Dr. Yen Sin! SWIFT AS a cobra, a long, gloved hand shot out. A black curtain flashed down over the window, and with a snarl of gears the car plunged away. Traile whirled, almost knocked Eric Gordon down.

"Get in!" he shouted above the sudden barking of police guns. He was under the wheel, engine started, when Glover raced up. The F.B.I. man lunged into the rear as Traile sent the car forward. Two or three harbor police were blazing away after the limousine. One man sent a bullet ricocheting from Traile's left front fender.

"Hold it!" Glover bawled at him.

The sedan skidded on the wet car-tracks, straightened under

Traile's deft handling. He twitched the spotlight. The limousine was careening northward into Seventh Street, and dimly he could see the other car just ahead. Eric, beside him, was tensely watching through one arc of the dual-wiper.

"Did you see him?" Traile rapped at the younger man.

"Did I? I'll never forget that face if I—" Eric broke off with a start. "You don't mean—"

"Right," said Traile, grimly. "The man in that car is Dr. Yen Sin!"

Eric's jaw dropped, and Glover swore in amazement. Traile crouched over the wheel, like some stern figure in bronze.

"Be ready. They'll try to lead us into a trap."

"I've three slugs left in this thirty-eight," Glover said fiercely.

Traile took out his automatic; thrust it into Eric's hand. "There's a fresh clip in the door-pocket beside you. We'll need it."

Eric hastily reloaded the weapon. Traile stared into the fog. He could barely see the fast-moving limousine, but he dared not close in for fear of a sudden trick by the driver. The thought had no more than passed through his mind when the other machine made a furious burst of speed. He pressed the throttle down, then jammed on the brakes with a muttered oath.

The limousine had made a reckless turn, was racing away at right angles. He sent the sedan thundering after it, the spotlight probing to find its ghostly bulk. The misty light soon fell on the car, but before he could decrease the gap the first machine dropped back to cut them off. Eric leaned out and fired.

"Get back!" Traile said swiftly. "Close the window!"

AS HE spoke, the other car swerved sharply to cross their path. A small, misshapen figure sprang up on the running-board, one gorilla-like arm raised. With a lightning turn, Traile sent the sedan toward the curb.

"Hold your breath!" he shouted.

The next instant something like a gilded puff-ball popped softly against the glass at his left. As the sedan hurdled the curbing, weird, shiny tendrils spread out, became a golden haze obscuring the whole left side of the car. He spun the wheel again. The sedan plunged along the walk, grazed a tree and bounced back into the street. At suicide speed, he raced on into the fog, until at last the eerie golden dust was sucked away.

"All right now," he flung tensely over his shoulder.

Both Eric and Glover let out explosive breaths. "For God's sake, what was it?" Eric burst out.

"*Ski muh*—the Corpse-Flower of Tibet!" Traile's dark eyes were searching the rear-vision mirror. "Thank Heaven we had warning. That was what the Chinese threw from the boat."

"You think it would have killed us?" Glover exclaimed hoarsely.

"In three seconds, if we had breathed that dust."

"By God, this is horrible!" Glover rasped. "Michael, we've got to wipe out Yen Sin!"

"We've a fighting chance, right now." Traile reached down and switched off the lights. "He's undoubtedly watching from the limousine, and when he sees our lights go out he may think we were killed and that the car crashed into something."

HE PEERED ahead. Even in the swift action of evading the other car, he had not taken his eyes from the limousine except for that quick glance at the mirror. It was keeping up its swift, dangerous pace through the fog. He followed tenaciously, averting collision with two or three other machines by hair-raising margins. Several angry pedestrians shouted at them as they swept past.

At Tenth Street, the limousine began a zigzag course, working toward Pennsylvania Avenue. Traile closed in, glued his eyes to the other car's tail-light.

"Any sign of that second machine?" he hurriedly asked Glover.

"No, we shook them off."

"I don't like the looks of it," Traile muttered. "It was too easy."

"Easy, hell!" said the F.B.I. chief. "I'd hate to have many nights like this."

The limousine swung into Fourteenth Street, its powerful headlights making two shimmering tunnels in the fog. Traile dodged around several other cars crawling at a slower pace. The theater traffic had all but snarled the avenue. The limousine shot between two cars, turned westward. Traile grazed one of the machines, swerved out to the car-tracks, hastily closing the gap.

"Get ready! I'm going to head them off."

He switched on his lights as they passed the Treasury and turned south into the Park. The shiny bulk of the limousine loomed up in the mist-white rays. His pulses gave a leap. There at the rear window had been a brief flash of yellow. The Invisible Emperor was trapped!

With a quick spurt, he drew abreast. The limousine swerved hastily toward the East side of the Ellipse. Traile pushed the throttle hard down, jerked the wheel. The other car's tires shrieked as he cut in front of it. He jammed on his brakes and the two cars slid to a halt, the limousine's bumper almost against a tree.

"Stay here!" he flung at Eric. Snatching his gun, he threw open the left-side door and raced around behind the sedan. Glover had already jumped out and dashed to the other side of the long limousine.

At the instant the two machines stopped, a dome-light had gone on within the limousine. Traile sprang forward, gun lifted. Then his tense look changed to stupefaction.

The malignant face, the yellow-robed figure of Dr. Yen Sin had vanished, and in his place was a pretty blond girl in a blue satin evening gown. No one else was visible except a hawk-faced chauffeur in livery who glared around from the driver's seat.

As Traile stood dazed, Glover came charging around from the other side, his belligerent face a picture of consternation.

"Did he come out this side?" he rasped.

Traile shook his head dumbly.

"Where the devil is he, then?" demanded Glover. "Don't tell me he's turned himself into a woman."

Traile wheeled toward the rear door of the limousine, but the girl rolled down the window before he could turn the knob.

"Would you mind explaining," she said in an icy voice, "by what right you stop a car of the British Embassy?"

Traile stared down at the crest on the side of the big limousine. It was the coat-of-arms of Great Britain. He looked up, gazed searchingly into the car. The girl drew back haughtily, the light gleaming in the spun-gold of her hair.

"If you are police, I will remind you that there is such a thing as diplomatic immunity—in case my driver has broken some minor traffic rule."

Traile's bronzed face was grim. "There is no immunity for murder."

A startled look came into her oddly luminous blue eyes. Then her rouged lips hardened. "You must be insane! Move your car and let me go on—or I shall report this outrage to the State Department."

"Ten minutes ago," Traile said coldly, "I saw an international criminal in this car. I did not see him leave."

"Ridiculous! Ten minutes ago, my car was in line approaching the marquee of the National Theater, where I was waiting, after the play."

Traile had come so close that he was stooping to peer inside. He fixed his glance on her brightly shining eyes. "And since when," he asked tonelessly, "has it been the custom to worship *Chandu* at the National Theater?"

A sudden pallor came into her face, and he saw the hawk-faced chauffeur stiffen.

"I don't know what you mean," she said in a low voice.

"Perhaps," he said slowly, "I should explain—to the British Ambassador."

He could see the mounting desperation in her eyes. She put out a jeweled hand pleadingly, then let it sink down at her side.

Her glance shifted abruptly past Traile, and from the corner of his eye he saw that Eric had climbed out and joined the group. His gaze was turned only a fraction of a second, but when he looked back at her he had a strange feeling that something had happened. She had a frightened expression, as though she were listening tensely.

"What is it you wish?" she asked him in an almost panicky voice.

"An explanation." His dark eyes bored into her. "Where is the man who was in this car?"

Her luminous eyes darted swiftly toward the chauffeur, then with a hasty movement she opened the door and stepped out.

"I'll submit to no more questions—I've told you that you've made a mistake." She gestured imperiously to the chauffeur. "Albert, get me a cab."

THE MAN jumped to the ground, but Glover caught the girl's bare arm as she tried to run past him. "No, you don't! Immunity or no immunity—you've got some explaining to do."

She wrenched her arm away with such force that her white satin cloak fell from her bare shoulders. She snatched it up before it touched the ground, but not in time to hide the mark on her other arm. There against the flesh were the outlines of talon-like fingers!

Traile leaped toward her as he saw where long fingernails had dug into her arm. "Yen Sin's hand made that mark! Where is he?"

As though in swift answer, a whistling sound came from directly behind him. He whirled toward the limousine, then

A beam of green fire
shot through his body.

sprang back in dismay. Velvety black smoke was swirling furiously within the car. In a twinkling, the glow from the dome-light was blotted out. The smoke poured from the opened door and billowed forward through the driver's compartment. In a moment more, the headlights were lost in an opaque cloud which rapidly hid the entire machine.

"Keep back—it may be poisonous!" Traile shouted at Eric and Glover.

Eric was sprinting around to get on the other side. Traile ran back to the sedan, pointed the spotlight into the whirling black cloud. Glover was dashing back and forth at the rear of the limousine, the .38 clutched in his hand. Traile looked around hurriedly.

"The girl! She's gone—and the chauffeur, too!"

"They ran right into that smoke!" grated the F.B.I. chief. "They must be in there."

"Eric!" Traile called out sharply. "Where are you?"

"Over this way," came Eric's muffled answer. "You can see part of the car from this side."

Traile strode around and joined him. The sluggish breeze was blowing some of the smoke away. He could see the doors as the black cloud began to evaporate. In a minute the smoke was gone, and the dome-light shone darkly through the smudged windows.

"Empty!" said Eric in an amazed voice.

Traile slowly nodded. "I didn't expect anything else. They simply ran through the cloud and out the other side."

"It stumps me," Glover said fiercely. "If it was Yen Sin who set off that stuff, where was he hidden? There's not enough room under the seat."

Eric grinned lopsidedly. "Maybe this 'Invisible Emperor' idea is straight dope."

"I don't believe he was ever in the car," snapped Glover. "You two just thought you saw him."

Traile silently bent over and looked at something on the floor. He picked it up, held it under the light. It was a gray silk glove, with strangely long fingers.

"Here's your answer," he said somberly. "See where the nails have cut at the tips? This glove came from the hand of Dr. Yen Sin."

CHAPTER 6
A GIFT TO CHINA

BEFORE AN apparently solid wall, at the end of a damp and musty passage, a tall figure had paused. He reached up, carefully pressed his long fingers against a spot above his head. A section of stone rotated silently on pivots. The man stooped, went through into a lighted chamber, and the stone closed behind him.

The room he had entered was furnished more luxuriously than is the usual Chinese manner. Soft amber lights shone on a divan, back of which was a red and gold screen. A thick Javanese rug covered the floor, and silken cushions were strewn around at the base of the walls. Beside a deep chair, lacquered in blood-red, was a stand on which lay a long-stemmed brass pipe, a spirit lamp, and a tin-foiled ball of opium. A bowl containing a gummy stick showed that some one had recently indulged in the devotional rite of Chandu. A woman's silver vanity case lay on a carved dressing-table nearby.

The man halted for an instant before the octagonal mirror, scrutinizing the sinister yellow face which looked back at him. The lights made hard shadows, intensifying the pitiless lines about his eyes and mouth. With no change of expression, he turned from the glass. Passing between portière curtains, he entered another room.

The contrast was complete. Bottles of chemicals, test-tubes, retorts, and all the equipment of a laboratory littered one side of the long chamber. Weapons of various kinds, boxes and cartons, and books on surgery and toxicology filled shelves across the room. Between, stood an acid-scarred table, and in a half-curtained recess was a makeshift operating-table on which lay a man's body.

The man had been bound there by straps, and gagged to prevent any outcry. A red-stained sheet was drawn carelessly over part of his body. His face was swollen and gruesomely dark. But the eyes were alive!

Dr. Yen Sin glanced at him without emotion. The tortured eyes of the dying man looked up at the other with a pitiful, frantic appeal. The Yellow Doctor smiled, calmly touched the man's sweating temples. He made a notation on a pad, went to a steel door which had once been part of a small vault. Fresh cement, where it fitted the wall, indicated that it had not been there long. He spun the dial, entered an unlighted chamber, and closed the door behind him.

There was a click, and a single light went on at one end of the room. It was suspended low, with a canted reflector which left most of the room in shadow. Beyond was a small, arched vestibule, of blackened and ancient brick. A slanting passage led downward at the right, and a closed door of new and heavy planking was visible on the left. On one side of the room was a couch, and beside it an opium layout such as had been in the other room. In the center of the room was a long table. A peculiar switchboard had been installed so that it lay flush with the table, its surface horizontal. A map of Washington had been cut and its sections placed around the four edges of the switchboard. Colored circles and checkmarks were numbered to correspond with sockets on the switchboard. A compact Dictaphone amplifier-box stood near an apparatus like a ticker-tape at the end of the table.

The Crime Emperor sat down before the switchboard, pressed a button. A green light glowed, and a sing-song voice spoke in mandarin dialect from the amplifier-box. Dr. Yen Sin replied curtly, then listened, frowning, to the hasty report of the unseen Chinese. Once, a furious look swept over his satanic countenance. It was gone in a second, leaving only a cold ferocity in his tawny eyes. When the report was finished, he leaned toward the grilled opening of the Dictaphone.

"Send her to me," he ordered.

"*Tche*, Master," the voice answered.

THE YELLOW DOCTOR sat back, tracing a finger across the edge of the map. A red light flickered twice on the switchboard. He touched a toggle. A harsh voice boomed from the amplifier.

"—I tell you, Mr. Secretary, this thing is a deadly menace!"

"I think you're unduly alarmed, Glover," came the impatient response. "If these Chinese killers are really at work in the capital, your agents should be able to clean up the situation in a day or so."

"But this Dr. Yen Sin—"

"I've already made inquiries at the Chinese Legation," said the impatient voice. "They've never heard of him, and they ridiculed the idea of this 'Invisible Empire' which has you so upset."

"Very well, sir," Glover's voice said stiffly. There was a click.

Dr. Yen Sin disconnected the tapped line. His thin lips held a mirthless smile. Suddenly a footstep sounded, haltingly, and a woman appeared in the arched vestibule. She was young, and beautiful with a strange, exotic allure, but her red lips had a pitiful droop and her dark eyes were wide with a haunting fear.

"You sent for me?" she said almost in a whisper.

The Yellow Doctor looked up with a feline smile. "Perhaps my instructions were not clear tonight?" he asked softly.

She stopped under the light, fearfully watching him. "I couldn't help it," she faltered. "Li Cheng misunderstood—"

The slanting eyes of Yen Sin seemed to reach out and draw her closer. She took a dragging step, halted, shivering.

"Because of your—error," the Crime Emperor pursued, silkily, "Michael Traile still lives."

"I was afraid to use *Shi muh*," she whispered. "I have always been afraid—"

Dr. Yen Sin raised his hand sharply. "Lies, my dear Sonya!" His silky voice had changed to a lashing tone. "You think sometime to escape me, because you always have avoided committing murder."

She shrank under the savage rasp of his words. He dropped a clenched hand on the table, then with an effort forced the rage from his voice.

"Fortunately, your espionage value to me saves you from the usual penalty. Torture might spoil your beauty."

Her face was slowly paling. The Crime Emperor's lips curled in a mocking smile.

"I am sending a message to China, a little gift from you to your father."

"No, no—not that!" she moaned. "Beat me—kill me—but don't torture him again!"

"A gift of fifty lashes," Yen Sin said gently. "And perhaps—the iron boot."

"No, for God's sake!" she cried wildly. "Have mercy on him. He has done nothing." Her voice broke in a sob. "He is old—it will kill him."

"My men will guard against that," said the Yellow Doctor suavely. "A live hostage is more valuable than a dead one."

She stumbled against the table, reached out toward him with a trembling hand. "Spare him—I will not forget again."

A light flickered on the switchboard. Dr. Yen Sin looked down, moved a toggle switch with the cool deliberation of a chess player.

"You may go, Sonya."

"Then—you will not torture him?" she said pleadingly.

He raised his head, and at the look which came into his terrible eyes she backed away. With a broken cry, she turned and went blindly from the room. Yen Sin pressed a button, leaned toward the Dictaphone.

"Report," he directed coldly.

"I am in position," a hoarse voice replied in Cantonese. "There have been no calls. The man named Traile has a visitor—a man a few years younger than he. Traile's manservant has brought them food—"

69

"You are sure you can not be seen?" Dr. Yen Sin interrupted swiftly.

"I have been careful, Master. The shutters are closed, as before, but I am looking down their slant."

"Let me know at once when the visitor leaves," Yen Sin commanded. "Also, be ready to advise Ling Ho as to the location of Traile's bedroom. We will wait until he is asleep."

"I believe, Master, he must sleep elsewhere," came the hurried reply. "There is no bedroom."

Yen Sin stared down at the glowing light on the switchboard.

"Then our plans must be changed—at once—before he can leave there. Listen carefully." He spoke rapidly for almost a minute. "And be certain," he ended with a sudden note of menace, "that you make no mistake."

"On my life, Master," came the hoarse whisper from the box.

There was a faint click, and the glowing light went out. Dr. Yen Sin sat back. His long fingers slowly tapped the arms of his chair.

CHAPTER 7
THE GREEN DEATH

MICHAEL TRAILE looked up from the depths of his big chair as Eric momentarily ceased his restless pacing.

"I swear," Eric said impetuously, "I don't see how you take it so easy after all that's happened."

"I want to put Yen Sin out of mind a few minutes, until my

brain is clearer. This is one of the times, old man, when I have to charge up the battery," Traile explained.

Eric stared down through the smoke from his pipe.

"Hanged if I hadn't forgotten that, with all this mess. You mean this is what you call a—"

"Relax-period?" Traile finished, as Eric hesitated. He nodded with an oddly lazy movement of his head. "That's it—this is my 'sleep.'"

"Well, why didn't you say so?" erupted the other man. "I'll get out of here—"

"No, I told you this was a safer place tonight. And don't worry about bothering me. It's my body that relaxes—not my mind. Although the old bean does clear up and work a little faster after one of these periods, when I've been under a strain like tonight."

Eric watched him curiously. Traile looked up with an amused expression in his dark eyes.

"You needn't act as though you were looking at a freak in some circus, you young cub!"

Eric grinned sheepishly. "Anybody'd think you were about a hundred, the way you talk."

Traile's tanned face clouded. "Sometimes I feel all of that, Eric." He gazed unseeingly before him a moment. "When I was just a kid, I used to wonder about it when people went to sleep. I thought they were sick. My parents finally had to let me know that I wasn't like other people. I didn't mind for a while—it seemed like a lark, doing a lot more than other youngsters—but later I realized what Fate had done to me. It's been a pretty lonely road."

Eric puffed vigorously at his pipe. "Maybe you ought to get married."

Traile smiled ironically. "I'm afraid no woman would care to put up with my eccentricities. I come and go at any hour—trek off to another country if I feel like it—"

"What a life," sighed Eric.

Traile glanced around his comfortably furnished, masculine living-room. "I'm sorry, but you'll have to sleep on that couch. Denny can bring up a blanket and some sheets from his room— he lives down in the servants' quarters of the apartment."

"Don't worry," said Eric. "I can sleep on a concrete floor. Darned if it doesn't seem funny, though—an apartment without any bedroom."

"I needed the space." Traile pointed through the well stacked library which adjoined the living-room. "Push that middle switch-button, and you'll get a glimpse of my junk-shop."

Eric complied, and lights went on in both the library and the room beyond it. The place was a maze, with *objects d'art,* unusual lamps, swords, carvings, and curios from a score of countries crowded together. A pair of skis stood beside a Moro kris and some hockey clubs. A rack of foreign costumes almost hid a gun cabinet. A jade Buddha on a carved teakwood table looked out ludicrously from under a gray wig which had been tossed over its head.

"What's the idea of that?" said Eric, grinning at the wigged Buddha.

The languid expression vanished from Traile's dark face. "I was using it as a wig-stand. That box at the side happens to be a theatrical make-up kit—a relic of one of my earlier hobbies. I've recently had good use for it."

His grim tone made Eric glance at him quickly.

"Yen Sin? Or don't you want to talk about it?"

Traile stood up, lit a cigarette. He seemed on the instant another man. The faint lines of strain about his mouth had gone. The lazy, far-off expression of his eyes had changed as by magic to a keen alertness.

"I've put you in a bad spot, Eric," he said crisply. "For your own protection, I'll have to explain my connection with this affair." He paused as the white-haired, kindly old manservant removed the small table on which he had served a midnight repast. When the old man had disappeared, he went on rapidly. "Three months ago, just after that incident of the Dragon's Shadow at Chefoo, I unwisely poked my nose into something I discovered at Shanghai. It finally led me into the Invisible Empire. Because I happened to know several dialects, and knew a little about changing my appearance, I was able to trick one of Dr. Yen Sin's most trusted agents. I attended a secret meeting of the Empire—that is, a meeting of Yen Sin's agents from several parts of the world. I was discovered at the last moment, but I managed to escape, and also to wreck one of his schemes."

Traile inhaled deeply several times, the muscles tightening in his tanned cheeks.

"Since then, they have constantly been after me. On the ship back, and on the way here from the Coast, I just escaped being murdered. I went to the State Department, convinced them of the danger from this unholy organization. They asked me to make up a secret unit to fight Yen Sin. I didn't like the idea of heading any group, or being tied down to red tape. So we compromised on a free-lance status."

He explained briefly the creation of the Q-Group, and its purpose to deceive the Crime Emperor. When he finished, he looked at Eric with worried eyes.

"You see? Yen Sin must already suspect that I am one of this supposed group. Now he'll think you're another of the five agents. You're in as much danger as I am."

Eric's ruddy face had lost some of its boyish look. His blue eyes met Traile's firmly. "Thanks for handing it out straight. But I'm not ordering any coffin yet."

Traile looked absently at the shuttered windows. "You'll have to be on your guard every minute. I can have John Glover assign a couple of agents—"

"I'm not going to have any bodyguard following me around," growled Eric. "If you don't mind, I'll stick along with you till we nab this yellow devil."

"Your company may be needing a new traveling inspector," Traile warned him.

"I'll risk it." Eric sucked fiercely at his pipe for a moment. "I don't see why we can't find where Yen Sin is hidden. There ought to be some clues in all this business tonight."

TRAILE DROPPED back into his chair. His face sobered in thought. "Some of it has cleared a little," he muttered. "I'm fairly certain that he had just arrived here. That thug was working

74

with other members of the Invisible Empire here, yet he hadn't delivered that letter. Either Yen Sin was on some other business, or he just reached here today."

"Then he's probably not hidden very well," exclaimed Eric. "We ought to get a lead a lot easier."

"No, he undoubtedly has had agents working here a month or more," said Traile. "He always has hide-outs prepared in advance. I'm positive there's a complete base in New York, which he hasn't occupied yet."

The old servant came in from his pantry. "Anything else, Mr. Michael, before I get the bedclothes?"

"No—yes, there is, too, Denny. Would you mind getting my file on Chinese codes?"

"Right away, sir," said Denny. He smiled at Eric. "If you don't mind waiting a few minutes more, Mr. Gordon?"

"Take your time," grinned Eric. "I'm not sleepy."

Traile was frowning into space.

"The characters on the shoulders of those Burmen must have been part of some very important message—something Yen Sin's agents in Asia wanted sent so that nobody could assemble it like written sections of a code. And the fact that Dr. Yen Sin himself took charge of the affair at the morgue proves it was doubly important. Glover was probably right—that man was drowned accidentally, and Yen Sin just heard that the body had been recovered. That thug must have sneaked in from the river side and killed the morgue attendant. He or another agent removed the message with acid, after copying it—unless they already had seen it before the man was drowned. And we showed up just in time to keep the Burman from escaping."

"That hooks up all right," nodded Eric. "But that limousine stunt has still got me going in circles."

Traile smiled wryly. "I'm afraid we were deceived by a very simple trick. There were two cars, remember."

"Yeh, but we would've seen him—"

"There was a second when the limousine spurted ahead. The other car dropped back, a little later, and tried to cut us off. In that second, with both machines parallel and before we caught up again, Dr. Yen Sin must have switched cars. He also must have given the girl some kind of smoke-bomb to throw out and blind us. She thought we'd been stopped when our lights went off. When we caught up, she decided to use it to escape further questions.

"Yen Sin's tricks aren't always so easily explained," Traile said grimly. "He has a habit of combining the mysticism of the East with the latest devices of the West, and with diabolical results."

Denny reentered the room, with a sheaf of papers in his hand. Traile got up quickly. "Ah, now we may get some idea of Yen Sin's purpose here."

He took from his pocket the wad of heavy paper which held the piece of skin from the thug's shoulder. He was unwrapping it when the telephone rang shrilly. Denny turned to the phone-stand near the window. Traile nodded, at the old man's inquiring glance.

"The usual answer."

Denny lifted the instrument.

"What number were you calling, please?"

There was a pause, then the receiver rattled out a reply which was audible in the hushed room. "I must talk to Mr. Traile, at once."

Traile's eyes narrowed sharply, for the "r" had had the slurred pronunciation of a Chinese. He took a step forward, as Denny put down the phone and moved back. Suddenly a faint gleam of metal showed down through the slanted shutters.

"Jump back!" he shouted at Denny. In the same moment he leaped sidewise toward the light-switch.

There was a hissing roar, and like a bolt of lightning, a beam of green fire shot clear through the shutters and bulletproof glass. Denny gave a tortured cry as the deadly flame burned into his body. For one awful second, that terrible scream rang through the room, then he tumbled to the floor.

TRAILE JABBED the switch-button as the green flame blared. The lights went out, but the green fire lit up the room with a dazzling glare. He had a swift glimpse of Eric, stumbling back, his hand before his face. Then the roaring emerald flame twitched toward the spot where he crouched.

He flung himself backward into the doorway, snatching the gun from his armpit holster. From under his shielding hand, he could see out into the night. The green fire had burned a huge hole in the shutters and melted a spot in the glass. Fifteen feet away, clinging to a telephone pole, was an ape-like figure. Above the stream of greenish flame which he was projecting into the room, showed the vicious features of a Chinese.

Traile threw himself down on one knee, fired just above the

green flame. The Oriental's face contorted in a spasm of pain. With a furious jerk, he whipped the beam down toward the kneeling man.

A terrific heat leaped out at Traile. He pumped two shots through the hole in the glass and dropped to the floor. With a violent sweep, the scorching green fire tilted up toward the ceiling. Then suddenly it snaked across to the window and disappeared from view.

Half dazed, Traile raised himself up. The Chinese had fallen from the pole. He could hear the man's howls of anguish from somewhere below. He jumped to the window with Eric at his elbow. The green fire was dying out at a spot near the foot of the pole. Two scurrying figures were carrying the wounded man toward a car half hidden in the misty alley. A fourth man snatched up something and followed the others, green sparks dropping from the object he had seized.

Traile leaned out and fired, oblivious to the excited shouts from nearby windows. The fourth man tripped, but was up in a flash. As Traile triggered his last shot, the machine jumped forward and plunged into the foggy night. He turned, pulled down a smoldering tapestry, beat out the flames which were consuming the shutters. Grimly ignoring the anxious queries of the other apartment dwellers, he beckoned to Eric and pointed to the pole. A lineman's telephone dangled from the wires.

"I've been living in a fool's paradise," he said savagely. "That devil was out there long enough to have killed both of us— instead of poor old Denny."

He knelt by the twisted form of the old man, his blurred eyes hardly noticing the charred remnants of the Chinese codes.

"Eighteen years of faithful service," he said huskily, "and now he dies in place of me."

Eric dropped his hand on the other man's shoulder. "You couldn't help it, Michael."

"I should never have let him stay with me!" rasped Traile. "I'm a marked man! You'd better clear out, Eric, before they get you, too."

"After all this?" said Eric harshly. "No, I'm sticking!"

Traile stood up to his full height, and for a moment his dark gaze burned into Eric's unflinching blue eyes. Then he slowly nodded. Above old Denny's body, their hands met in a stern and silent pact.

CHAPTER 8
THE EYES OF THE MIKADO

IT WAS eleven o'clock, and the Japanese Embassy ball was in full swing. Guests of a dozen nationalities—uniformed officers, women in colorful gowns, and diplomats in somber evening garb made a picturesque, gala scene. The soft strains of an orchestra blended with the buzz of conversation, reducing it to a pleasant hum. But for at least two men in that gathering, there was an ominous undercurrent to the flow of gayety.

"If anything's going to happen," muttered Eric Gordon, "I wish it would hurry up. I'm getting a case of the jitters."

"Not so loud," warned Michael Traile. He moved back a little farther into the subdued light of the reception hall. "We don't know how many members of the Invisible Empire are here tonight."

Eric looked around, an uneasy expression on his ruddy face. A middle-aged Japanese, with the decoration of the Rising Sun distinguishing his evening clothes, gave him a brief glance in passing.

"Say," Eric whispered, as soon as the man was out of hearing, "that's twice I've seen him looking me over. What if he's found out we're here under fake names?"

Traile carelessly lit a cigarette, the flare of the lighter throwing his deeply tanned face into sharp relief.

"Don't worry about Nikki. He's the First Secretary of the Embassy—the one who knows about us."

"Well, I still don't like it," complained Eric. "When he introduced us to the Ambassador, I swear he looked as though he thought I were a crook or something."

Traile gazed idly over the throng in the ballroom.

"We had to work it that way," he said, with lips which seemed hardly to move. "Paul Raville—my chief contact man at the State Department—suddenly got a lead on the Vaughan girl at the British Embassy. He and Glover both have had men watching her after that night—also the chauffeur—even though diplomatic immunity has forced them to play a hands-off game. She hadn't stirred out of the Embassy until this afternoon, then she went for a drive through Rock Creek Park. Bill Shaw—the F.B.I. agent here tonight—saw another car slow down beside hers, evidently for a brief message. Shaw tried to follow the other car, but lost it in downtown traffic. An hour later, a request from the British Embassy came through to the State Department, for last-minute invitations to the Japanese affair tonight. They're often arranged that way. Raville told me, and we both decided it was a logical place for this Iris Vaughan to meet an agent of Yen Sin without our knowing who the agent was. She could talk or dance with two or three dozen people—"

"Then why aren't we watching her now?" demanded Eric.

"Because she knows both of us. Bill Shaw and Lieutenant Fuller—Naval Intelligence—are keeping her spotted, and so is Raville."

Traile motioned casually with his hand, as though flicking an ash from his cigarette. Eric followed the faint gesture, saw an American naval officer in formal mess jacket with gold epaulets, as the man strolled past with a quiet, scholarly looking civilian. Fuller glanced sidewise at the two men in the wide doorway, but Raville made no sign of recognition.

"They were already on the State Department list," Traile explained in an undertone. "This Vaughan woman wouldn't suspect them, if she checked the final Japanese invitation list—which the British Embassy could get without trouble. That's why we're using false names—and keeping out of the limelight."

Eric grinned crookedly. "I hope you know what you're doing. I'd hate to be pinched with this fancy gat under my coat. They'd probably take me for a gangster."

A shrewd-faced man in evening clothes appeared from a room farther along the hall. He approached them with ill-disguised haste.

"Here comes Shaw," whispered Eric. "He looks excited about something."

SHAW FISHED a cigarette from his pocket. "Could I borrow a light?" he jerked out for the benefit of anyone listening. Then, as Traile took out his lighter, he went on hurriedly under his breath. "I just got wise to something queer. That blonde's danced with only four men—and they've all four disappeared!"

Traile's dark-brown eyes narrowed a fraction of an inch. "Who were they?"

"The one that brought her—the Limey; two foreign-looking birds—I think one was an Italian; and the Jap that introduced everybody—"

"Nikki?" Traile barely hid a start. "Good Heavens, if he's one of the members of the Invisible Empire—"

"Raville wants to see you," Shaw cut in. "He's back in the second room."

Traile pocketed his lighter. "Eric, you stay here and keep your eyes open for anything peculiar. I'll be back in a minute."

Shaw went part of the way with him. "I'm going to sneak around and see if I can find where those birds went."

Traile nodded. Shaw turned, started through the crowded buffet-room. Traile found Raville waiting with a strained look on his scholarly face.

"Michael," whispered the State Department man, "there's something sinister happening here."

"I know," Traile said grimly. "I've felt it ever since I came in."

"This is more than feeling," Raville said tensely. "Lieutenant

82

Fuller has vanished. He was standing here at my elbow one moment—then he was gone. And I found this by the portières."

He held out a white dress glove of the type worn by naval officers. Across the back were four thin golden streaks, as though made by fingers dipped in gilt. Traile fairly snatched the glove from Raville's hand, as the State Department man started to raise it to his nostrils.

"What's the matter?" Raville said in amazement."

"It's *Shi Muh* again," Traile groaned. "If you'd sniffed that—" He whipped out his handkerchief, folded the glove tightly within it, avoiding the gilded section. "Better go to the smoking-room and wash your hands," he said swiftly. "I'll wait here."

A little pale, Raville hurried out of the room. Traile looked down searchingly at his own hands, then stepped to the doorway where the portières hung. It opened on a wide hall, with a circular stairway on the left, and doors to the private Embassy rooms along at the right. A cross-corridor led away at right angles. Traile stared down at the thick rug. Near the portières there was a rumpled spot.

There were only two people in the hall, which was well removed from the public rooms. One was an undersized Japanese, evidently a minor attaché, and the other a girl in an ivory-colored evening gown. He had only a glimpse of the girl's back as she entered the hall leading toward the ballroom. He was about to steal behind the Japanese and into the cross-corridor, when two people emerged from the side door to the buffet-room. He jumped back out of sight.

One of the two was Iris Vaughan.

From the concealment of the portiéres, he hastily surveyed her companion. The man was old, and his stooped form was clad in an obsolete but neatly pressed Russian uniform of the Czarist regime. His snowy head was bent, and even with the guiding hand of the blond girl at his side he fumbled his way with a cane, in the unmistakable manner of the blind. His wrinkled face was half turned, so that Traile had only a brief glance before the two figures disappeared in the corridor.

THE JAPANESE attaché had looked at them perfunctorily and then turned toward the circular stairway. Traile stepped out quickly and stopped him.

"Pardon me," he said, "I'm Mr. Lane, of the State Department. Can you tell me the name of the old Russian officer who just went by?"

The Japanese looked at him with surprise.

"But, Mr. Lane, it was your department which requested the invitations for him and his daughter—Duke Sergius Damatri and his daughter, Sonya."

"Oh, yes," Traile covered up carelessly, "I recall the names— but I had never seen the Duke and I knew that wasn't his daughter."

The attaché bobbed his head, smiled and went on. He was hardly out of sight before Traile was hurrying down the corridor between the rows of offices. Iris Vaughan and the blind old Russian were nowhere in sight. Traile halted, midway of the hall. At the blind man's slow pace, it hardly seemed possible they could have gone much farther than the third office.

He was about to try the knob of the nearest door when a

thin streak of light appeared under the next door on the left. He tiptoed closer, listened, but could hear nothing. A quick glance up the corridor showed him that no one was watching. Thrusting his hand under his coat, he cautiously turned the knob.

The door swung open silently, revealing a luxuriously furnished study. It appeared to be empty. Traile gave the door a hard push to be sure that no one was hiding behind it. It stopped with a soft thud against a rubber block. He stepped inside, closed the door, darting a quick glance about the room.

An enormous picture rug covered the floor. Book-shelves ranged on three sides, except where a gold-framed, full-length portrait of the Mikado stood in the middle of the longer wall. A shaded light shone down from the top of the picture. The only other light came from a small lamp on the library desk.

There was no one behind the desk, nor was there any other hiding-place, yet Traile had a sudden feeling of menace. He moved silently toward the door to the next room, the soft rug deadening his steps. Abruptly, he swung around. In that dead stillness there had been a faint scraping sound. He stared about him a moment, then leaped back with a stifled exclamation.

The eyes of the Mikado were suddenly alive!

As he sprang back, the eyes of the man behind the picture took on a fierce glitter. A faintly hissed command was audible through the peep-holes where the painted eyes had been. Traile hurled himself to one side, just as a small metal tube protruded from the left eye.

There was a click, and a tiny steel needle whizzed past his

head. Before the hidden man could aim again, Traile raked his gun down over the shifting tube. With a muffled clink, the tube fell to the floor. A voice snarled a Chinese oath from behind the portrait, then something slid over the peep-holes and again the painted eyes of the Mikado looked down upon him.

Traile swiftly pressed against the painted face, but a solid surface met his hand. There was only a tiny rip where the spring-gun had torn the canvas. All sound behind the picture had ceased. Keeping his gun poised, he hastily felt over the edge of the frame with his other hand. He had covered the right side, and was beginning to feel along the left when from out in the corridor he heard voices.

He wheeled and ran to the other end of the room. The door to the corridor started to open. Hurriedly, he opened the connecting door to the next room and stepped on through. There was a gasp. He spun around, closing the door behind him.

In the center of the dim-lit office he had entered stood Iris Vaughan. A few feet away was the blind Russian duke, half-surrounded by four snarling dacoits. At sight of Traile's gun, one of the Burmen made a lightning jerk for his knife.

"Stand still!" Traile grated out in Burmese.

THE MAN jumped at sound of his native tongue. Slowly, his hands went up. The blond girl started to run toward the door. One of the dacoits caught her arm. She tripped, bumped against the old Russian. The blind man took a tottering step, fumbling with his cane.

"Where are you, my dear?" he said harshly. "Take me away from these—"

From the room Traile had just quitted came a short, angry cry. He went rigid. It was Eric's voice.

He leaped backward, feeling for the knob. In the same instant, the blind Russian swiftly straightened. The closed lids under his craggy white brows flashed open. An icy chill went up Traile's spine, as he saw those terrible eyes.

The man before him was Dr. Yen Sin!

Even through the wrinkled make-up which hid the yellow skin, he could see the Satanic outlines of that diabolical face. As he caught the murder-light in those slitted eyes, he hastily swerved his gun.

"Get back!" he rasped.

The heavy cane was halfway raised in Yen Sin's gloved hand. The Yellow Doctor froze, glaring over the stick. Then slowly his lips curled into a mocking smile.

"So, Mr. Traile, we meet again."

Traile's eyes drilled into those of the Crime Emperor.

"Not a move, you yellow devil!"

Something flickered in the tawny eyes staring into Traile's. "Someday, my friend, you will regret that."

The brief cry from the other room had ended in stark silence. Desperately, Traile felt behind him for the door, his eyes never leaving the mocking face of Yen Sin. Behind the Crime Emperor, the girl and the dacoits were like blurred figures on a back-drop.

Traile's left hand touched the knob. But even as he grasped it, the door was swiftly opened from the other side. He sprang out of the way. It was barely a second, but in that instant Yen

Sin flicked the head of the cane to his lips. With horror, Traile saw the black hole in the end. The cane was a blow-gun!

In a frantic leap, he threw himself side-wise and fired. The bullet crashed through the side of the cane, tore it from Yen Sin's hand. Before he could fire again, a dark figure hurtled through the doorway. Two clawing hands closed around his throat, and he plunged to the floor with the other man on his back.

The dacoits darted in like hungry rats. A heel came down with grinding force on his right hand, and a savage kick drove the breath from his body. Then above the panting snarls of the Burmen, Yen Sin's voice crackled out a fierce command. The dacoits jumped up, and Traile dazedly heard them run from the room. The choking hands relaxed their hold on his throat. He was aware, though his eyes were closed, that the Yellow Doctor was hastily bending over him.

SUDDENLY, YEN SIN'S talon-like fingers pressed at a spot at the back of his neck. A terrific pain shot through his head, as though his brain were bursting. A cry rose to his lips, but his numbed throat made it only a tortured gasp. Paralyzed, he lay there like a dead man.

"Have you killed him?" he heard the girl ask in a trembling voice.

"No, he is merely unconscious," the Crime Emperor said harshly. "A less easy death awaits him."

Traile heard someone run through from the other room.

"The shot was not heard, Master," a man said in breathless Cantonese.

"Obviously not," Dr. Yen Sin replied curtly, "or the man at the lights would have mistaken it for the signal."

"Everything is ready," the man reported tensely. "We had to seize the other American—he recognized Sonya and followed her."

"Where is he now?"

"With Li Cheng, Master. Li Cheng is going to kill him."

"The stupid fool!" rasped Dr. Yen Sin. "Doesn't he see this is a chance to complete my plan? Come!"

Traile heard the two men move quickly toward the other room.

"What about me?" Iris Vaughan said in a panicky voice.

"Remain here," ordered Yen Sin. "I shall return at once."

"But if this man should recover?" she exclaimed, alarmed.

"There is no danger," the Yellow Doctor said impatiently. "The sleep center of his brain is inhibited. He will not awake until I release the pressure."

The connecting door clicked shut. Traile lay motionless, striving fiercely to force strength back into his numbed body. Already there was a prickling along his spine as the temporarily paralyzed nerves resumed their functions. His childhood injury had saved him from unconsciousness. He knew now what he had always suspected—that not even sheer agony, nor a stunning blow, could blot out his wakeful brain. Death was the only sleep he would ever know.

And with a driving grimness he realized that that sleep might not be far off. Dr. Yen Sin might return at any second. He listened intently, heard the girl's soft footsteps on the rug. A latch clicked—she was trying the lock of the main door to the office. He opened his eyes to a bare slit. Her back was turned. He tried to sit up, but the movement was leaden, slow. He flashed a look toward the table a few feet away. If he could pull himself up by grasping one of the legs....

Then he saw his gun, where the butt of it showed at the farther end of the table. The sight gave him a sudden spurt of energy. He gripped the table, was almost to his feet when the girl turned and saw him. With a lunge, he scooped up the weapon. She gave a stifled cry, shrank back, deathly white.

"Oh, God!" she moaned. "Don't kill me!"

Traile's dark eyes burned into hers over the lifted gun. "Unlock that door," he said in a harsh whisper.

She obeyed, her hand shaking on the latch. At his gesture, she opened the door and backed into the hall.

"Turn around and stand still!" he ordered.

She pivoted as though to comply, then ran wildly up the hall. Traile swore under his breath. His legs were not yet steady enough for hasty pursuit. He swung around, grimly started toward the connecting door. He had hardly taken a step when from somewhere near he heard a muffled shout. He wheeled, reached the hall with quickening steps.

Abruptly, the roar of a heavy-caliber pistol boomed through the rear of the building. Up near the front of the hall, a woman's voice screamed. Then all the lights went out.

Feeling his way along the wall, Traile headed toward the direction of the shot. A hubbub had arisen at the front of the building. In a moment the orchestra swept into a loud fox-trot, drowning the clamor of voices. As the lights flashed on, Traile saw a door open at his right. He shot a hurried glance inside, then stood there, appalled.

Sprawled over a desk, blood pouring from a revolver-shot in his side, was Nikki. And toppled across his body, a Navy Colt .45 gripped in his hand, was Lieutenant Fuller!

CHAPTER 9
TUNNEL OF TERROR

HORRIFIED, TRAILE stepped into the room, his eyes racing over the scene. Nikki's brown hands were locked in the naval officer's throat, and Fuller's mess-jacket was stained red from the blood of the Japanese. The floor was littered with papers, and on the wall beyond the desk a wall-panel had been slid back, exposing a small, round safe. The door of the safe was open. A window was raised, and one pane broken.

A flood of dismay swept over Traile as he realized the situation. Running feet sounded in the hall. He dashed across the office, his consternation lending him new power. If he were caught there....

The side door of the office was flung open just as he reached it. His heart sank. It was Ambassador Okada!

Okada stood for a second in blank amazement, his black eyes dilating behind his heavy glasses. "Nikki murdered!" he said hoarsely. "Murdered by an American officer!"

Several Japanese officials and Embassy guards ran into the room from the hall. They halted, staring at the dead men. Behind

Okada, Traile saw Raville gazing at the scene. The State Department man had a sick, stunned look.

"Nikki murdered!" the Ambassador said again, stupidly. Then for the first time his eyes fell on the papers which littered the floor. He whirled, and all the blood rushed from his face as he saw the opened safe. He sprang around toward Raville with a choked cry of fury.

"American treachery!" he burst out "You accept our hospitality—to steal our secrets!"

"Wait!" Traile broke in. "This is all a frame-up—this officer didn't kill Nikki!"

Okada spun around fiercely. "You are another spy! Nikki told me you were here under an assumed name—now I know why!"

"You've got to listen!" Traile said tautly. "Even now it may be too late!"

"Too late for your lies!" snarled Okada. "A child could see that this is a conspiracy directed by your Government!"

Traile tried to break in, but there was a sudden commotion outside the building, then an Embassy guard appeared from the rear hall, forcing a disheveled figure along at gun-point.

"Shaw!" groaned Raville. "Good Lord, man, how did you get mixed up in this?"

"I saw one of those four men," Shaw said thickly. "I followed him outside—somebody knocked me out, in the dark."

"I found him under this broken window," asserted the Japanese guard, glaring at Shaw. "There was an Embassy envelope beside him—but it was empty."

Traile had edged back beside Raville as attention was drawn to Shaw. "I'm going to break for it," he whispered.

"My God, no!" Raville said hoarsely. "They'll take it as proof that you're guilty."

"I can't help it," Traile said in a tense undertone. "Unless we get Yen Sin, this thing may mean war!"

He slipped back into the other room, but a sharp-eyed Japanese saw him. *"Goran nasai!* Look there!" he shouted. "The spy is escaping!"

TRAILE RACED out into the hall. At the farther end, three attachés were holding back the curious throng. As Traile dashed toward the study, the three Japanese broke into shouts of alarm. He jerked open the study door, slammed it and locked it in the faces of the pursuing guards. There was no one in the room. He ran across and saw that the other room also was deserted. He locked the connecting door as he hastily turned back into the study. The light was still lit over the portrait, but only the painted eyes of the Mikado looked out at him.

He took out the gun he had pocketed as Okada appeared. Hurriedly, he felt along the left edge of the heavy gold frame, then underneath. The hall door was trembling under a rain of blows. In desperation, he drove the butt of his gun against the painted eyes. Something gave with a ripping of canvas, then he saw that he had loosened a movable section on which the eyes were painted. He hammered furiously, and in a few seconds had torn a triangular hole in the picture, almost destroying the face of the Mikado.

The light at the top of the portrait shone in through the

jagged opening. He stiffened. A dim shape had moved through the light. He flattened himself against the wall, but no attack came. The Japanese guards were pounding madly at the hall door, and he knew the lock would give at any moment. He took another swift look through the hole.

This time he could see a man crouching on the floor of a small vault. In a quick glance he spied hinges at the right side of the huge frame. A rod with a coiled spring around the left end passed horizontally near the top of the portrait. He clawed at the spot where the rod seemed to end. A round piece of the frame, hardly larger than a dime, gave under his fingers, and with a low click the portrait swung open.

Behind him, wood splintered as the guards kicked a panel from the door. He sprang around the opening portrait, his automatic poised for action. A fairly large vault, evidently built to hide bulky documents and other secret objects, met his swift gaze. A sliding steel door had been pushed into a niche at the left. By the light which had been above the picture he saw a wild confusion of papers, letters and maps.

But his eyes rested only a second on the vault itself. The man on the floor was slowly getting to his feet. Traile leaped, rammed his gun into the other's side.

"Raise your hands!" he clipped out.

The command was half lost in a crash as the hall door burst open. The man swayed, jerked around into the light. Traile's gun dropped to his side.

"Eric!" he cried. "Thank God—I was afraid they'd killed you!"

"I thought they were going to," Eric said huskily. "But they ran—"

"Arrest them!" the furious voice of Okada broke in.

Traile whirled, and Eric looked out dazedly at the infuriated Japanese. Two guards jumped forward to obey the Ambassador's orders, but Paul Raville interposed with a frantic plea.

"Please wait, Your Excellency! I can explain everything."

"Silence!" Okada burst out. "I will listen to no more lies. I shall cable Tokyo at once, that my First Secretary was murdered on Embassy ground and that the Embassy secret files have been rifled by American agents!"

Raville's face blanched. "Good Heaven!" he moaned. "Don't you realize what it will mean?"

"You should have thought of that sooner," Okada flung back. He jerked around toward the opened vault, then his already blazing eyes lit with a mad glare.

"*Yaso Kirisuto!*" he screeched. "They have tunneled in from underneath—the code dispatch box is gone!"

TRAILE LOOKED, startled. One of the guards had produced a flashlight, and its probing rays were resting on a square hole which had been cut in the floor at the rear of the vault. Okada sprang past the guard, clutched Eric fiercely.

"Where is it?" he shouted. "Where have you thieves taken it?"

Eric threw him off angrily. "Don't call me a thief, if you don't want a sock in the—"

"Your Excellency!" Traile hastily interrupted. "We're letting the real criminals escape! The man who engineered this scheme is Dr. Yen Sin!"

The Ambassador gave a start. Traile swiftly pressed his advantage.

"We were following an agent of the Invisible Empire—we hoped to trap the doctor by watching her here. But it was worse than I dreamed. Yen Sin and at least six of his agents were here ten minutes ago!"

Okada's eyes wavered, then shot back to Eric Gordon. "More lies! This American was in the vault—"

"Yen Sin left him there to trick you," Traile insisted. "Lend me these guards—we'll follow the tunnel."

"No! It is you who are trying to trick me!" Okada turned with a furious dignity. "Mr. Raville, I will give you twenty-four hours—till midnight tomorrow—to prove that Yen Sin had any connection with this. But these men must remain prisoners here!"

"But they're the only ones who know anything about him," protested Raville.

"I have spoken." Okada motioned to the guards. "Arrest them."

He stepped back from the vault. The guard with the flashlight reached out to seize Traile's arm. Traile's hand shot to the guard's wrist. The flashlight dropped to the floor, and the Japanese went sailing out into the study. Two other guards leaped into the vault. Eric Gordon swung from the hip, and with a howl of pain the first man bounced backward. Traile caught the second guard squarely under the jaw. Before his man had struck the floor, he was whisking the steel door out of its niche. Okada let out a scream of pure rage. Raville stood aghast.

"Traile, for God's sake—have you lost your mind?" came his frenzied cry.

"This is the only way!" Traile shot back. The door slammed shut, and he saw the lock-bar fall into place. He turned quickly to Eric, who had picked up the flashlight. "It'll take them a minute to get the key. Come on."

"What are we going to do?" Eric exclaimed.

"First, see that we're not going right into another trap," Traile answered grimly. He took the flashlight, pointed it down into the tunnel. It had obviously been dug within the last few hours. Fresh earth and broken pieces of the cement floor were trampled together a few feet below the hole. The passage led down steeply into blackness.

"They lit out in a hurry," Eric muttered. "I don't think you'll find anyone."

"You can't be sure of anything, where that yellow fiend is concerned," Traile said in a lowered voice. He dropped into the tunnel. Holding the torch at one side, he turned the rays down into the passage. Nothing was visible for a hundred feet, at which point the tunnel leveled out. With Eric close behind, he started downward.

"I wish I had my gun," Eric said uneasily. "They copped mine."

"I'm not planning to tackle them without help," Traile answered, "Okada will have a dozen men chasing after us in a minute or two. We'll keep just far enough ahead to lead them to Yen Sin's hide-out. Even if he has flown, we ought to find some proof that he was involved."

"And if he hasn't flown, we'll catch hell from both sides," grunted Eric.

THEY HAD reached the spot where the tunnel flattened. The last half of the slanting passage had gradually widened, and the level stretch showed evidence of more careful digging. Traile twitched the flashlight.

"They must have had it all ready for breaking through, so they could connect with the vault in a couple of hours."

"I'm still going around in circles," Eric said glumly. "Everything happened so fast after I saw that girl—"

"So one lesson wasn't enough?" Traile asked drily.

"She didn't lead me into this," Eric said in a dogged voice. "She didn't even know I was following her—until three Chinks grabbed me in that room. One of them would have knifed me if she hadn't stopped him. Then Yen Sin came in and told them to keep me in the vault. They kept me, all right—just about choked, until after that shot. Then the whole outfit dashed into the vault and down this tunnel."

"The Vaughan woman, too?" cut in Traile.

"No—but I saw the other one. Yen Sin was right behind her. She acted as though she were trying to escape from him."

"From a charge of complicity in murder, you mean," rapped Traile. "They killed Nikki and Fuller, made it look as though Fuller murdered Nikki…. Listen!"

He switched off the light, and they stood there tensely.

"I don't hear anything," whispered Eric.

"It was up ahead," Traile said under his breath. "It sounded like a groan."

They waited a few moments in the dark. From back at the vault, angry voices suddenly were audible.

"We can't let them catch up yet," Traile said swiftly.

He pressed the flashlight button, kept it blinking as they hurried on. In about sixty feet the newly dug passage ended, opening into a tunnel of quite evident age. The floor was hard-packed, and the sides and roof were shored in places with old, musty timbers. Traile warily threw the beam along the passage. A half-rotted door stood partly open, a few yards to the left. The blackened floor was spotted with new earth which had been carried from the new tunnel. To the right of the junction, the old passage made a curve and then forked into two branches.

"Look!" exclaimed Eric. "They must've gone this way."

He sprang forward and picked up a jeweled ear-ring. As he straightened, his shoulder touched the old door. It moved an inch or two, grating on rusty hinges.

"That was the sound I heard," whispered Traile.

"Someone must be just ahead of us," Eric said in a hoarse answer.

Traile pointed the flashlight toward the ground. "A woman's sharp heels would have left some mark. That ear-ring was dropped there to mislead us."

He turned hastily as the voices of the pursuing Japanese became louder. They ran back to the fork, and again he swiftly inspected the ground. There were faint tracks of fresh earth on the floor of the left tunnel.

"Be ready to run!" he clipped at Eric "I'm going to make sure they follow us."

He wheeled, holding the torch away from him. Fifty feet away, the first Japanese plunged out of the Embassy passage. He dashed toward the rusty door, then whirled at Traile's shout. Five or six more brown men had poured from the newly dug tunnel. They all spun around at the sound of Traile's voice.

"This way!" he shouted, waving the light at one side. ONE OF the guards leveled his gun as he ran forward. Traile leaped back. But the shot never came. Without the slightest warning, there was a blast of flame and with a roar the timbered roof crashed down on the ill-fated guard. The explosion hurled Traile backward to the ground. A great cloud of smoke and dust belched out, and the shrieks of the trapped Japanese were drowned in a dull thunder, like the sound of an avalanche.

Cascading earth rolled into the branch tunnel as Traile staggered to his feet. Eric Gordon clutched at his arm.

"Michael! Are you hurt?"

"No," said Traile dully. "But those poor wretches—"

He swung the torch. Through the smoky dust a pile of earth and broken timbers was dimly visible. Of the Embassy guards there was not the slightest trace. The silence was appalling.

"Maybe some of them are safe on the other side," Eric said huskily.

Traile shook his head. "I'm afraid not. That bomb was planted to catch everyone within forty feet of the junction. It must have been set off by someone beyond that old door."

"Good Lord!" Eric suddenly groaned. "They'll think we did it—that we had it all planned!"

Traile nodded, his bronzed face grim. "Our only hope is to capture Yen Sin. And now there's hardly a chance in a thousand."

He had turned the light, probing the darkness of the branch tunnel. It was old, and timbered like the one which had just caved in. As they started on, the ominous thought came to him that this, too, might be mined. He looked over his shoulder at Eric, then changed his mind. There was no use to burden Eric with that haunting fear. Better, if it came, that it be over quickly. He carefully took out his handkerchief and, leaving it folded, covered the lens of the flashlight.

"Where do you suppose this leads?" Eric asked in a low tone, as Traile pointed the dimmed light ahead.

"I don't know, but it's evidently one of the old, forgotten tunnels. There are dozens of them underneath the Capital, most of them farther downtown. Some have caved in, and others have never been explored. Yen Sin's agents must have learned that this one led close to the Japanese Embassy."

"I don't see how they knew where to hook up with that vault," said Eric.

Traile peered cautiously around a turn in the passage.

"I think Nikki is the answer to that," he said as they went on. "He must have been caught in the Doctor's web. He undoubtedly helped in the preparations tonight—not dreaming his death was part of the scheme."

"And we're shut in here with that devil!" Eric said harshly.

"Not so loud," cautioned Traile. "There's another turn ahead."

They tiptoed forward in silence. The dim light of the covered torch fell on a sagging beam at the right. Traile hurried past, was almost to the turn when his straining ears caught a sound which was not made by their own footsteps. He spun around, then his heart seemed to jump into his throat.

Leaping toward Eric's back, his dagger fiercely lifted, was the giant figure of Li Cheng!

"Drop, Eric—drop!" Traile shouted madly.

CHAPTER 10
THE FLAMING CIRCLE

WITH A startled cry, Eric threw himself flat. The huge Chinese tripped over him and plunged headlong, his dagger jabbing into the ground. His heavy body had fallen across Eric, driving the breath from the other man's lungs. Traile hurled himself forward, sent the dagger flying with a furious kick. Li Cheng's huge hands shot out. Traile sprang side-wise, but one clutching hand gripped his right leg. He came down with a thud.

The impact jerked his gun from his hand. Li Cheng snatched at the weapon. Eric, pinned down by the huge man's enormous bulk, knocked it out of reach with a frantic sweep of his hand. Li Cheng made a vicious jab at Eric's eyes with two spread fingers. Traile struck at his arm, and the Oriental's fingers drove like a blunt fork into Eric's throat.

Eric collapsed with a moaning gasp. Traile was bent over backward, trying to reach his pistol. With a swift movement,

Li Cheng threw him clear over onto his back. One long yellow arm flashed out to the side and the huge Oriental retrieved his dagger.

Traile frantically rolled his head. His left hand was free—but the gun was hopelessly out of reach. He jerked wildly in the effort to wriggle loose. Li Cheng lurched against the wall of the passage, his descending dagger tearing through Traile's sleeve. His fiendish grin changed to a snarl. His grip at Traile's neck tightened as he yanked the knife from where it had caught.

Something hot had touched Traile's hand as he made that last wild effort. His eyes flicked toward the flashlight. A sudden hope swept over him. Fuller's glove had dropped from the half-unfolded handkerchief.

His snatching fingers closed on the gilt-stained cloth. Li Cheng's arm whirled upward with the knife. Desperately, Traile thrust the glove up at the Oriental's face. Li Cheng's head whipped back, and the flashing dagger started down. But with a spasmodic jerk, it stopped in mid-air. Li Cheng gave a strangled scream. The knife fell from his writhing fingers. A horrible, whistling groan escaped from his lips. He lunged to his feet, his slant eyes bulging in mortal terror.

For a second more he stood there, hands clawing his face in a frenzied attempt to wipe away the deadly golden dust. Then his knees buckled, and he sprawled in a lifeless heap.

Traile dragged his pinioned legs from under Li Cheng's body and hurriedly bent over Eric. The younger man sat up, tenderly rubbing his throat.

"Judas!" he said in a hoarse and painful whisper. "I thought I'd been stabbed."

"You didn't miss it by far," Traile told him grimly.

Eric managed a feeble grin. "Lord, I thought the tunnel had caved in again when that big lout fell on me."

"He's done his last killing." Traile's dark eyes flitted to Li Cheng's crumpled form. "For once, I'm thankful for *Chi Muh*."

He helped Eric to his feet, picked up his gun and the flashlight. He calmly wiped his hands on Li Cheng's sleeve, made sure that none of the golden dust of the "Corpse Flower" remained.

Eric stared back into the passage. "Say, maybe they're in that other branch passage," he whispered.

"No, I think Li Cheng was left as a rear-guard. He was probably the one who set off the bomb, but he must have been in the right branch-tunnel instead of where I thought."

Traile handed him the pistol and took the dagger Li Cheng had dropped. "Come on. I've a sudden dislike for this tunnel." As he led on ahead, he kept the flashlight behind him, pointed down at the ground so that he moved in shadow. The tunnel made another curve—and abruptly ended. Traile instantly switched off the light, but his momentary glimpse had been sufficient.

"There's a flight of steps leading up to a trap-door," he whispered to Eric. "We'll have to make it in the dark."

THEY CREPT forward without making a sound. After a minute, Traile's groping hand touched the cold stone steps. Eric

104

came to a halt at his elbow, breathing tensely. Traile turned, put his lips to Eric's ear.

"I'm going to crawl up under the trap and listen. If I'm caught, you run for it!"

He silenced Eric's whispered protest, cautiously climbed up the steps. He had stuck Li Cheng's dagger at the side of his belt, and the unlighted torch was in his left hand. He crouched just under the trap, listening intently.

Not a sound came from above. He turned his head to the side, placed his ear against the cold, dank surface of the trap. He waited for five minutes, but nothing broke the tomb-like silence. He felt around the trap. It seemed solid enough to prevent any light from shining through. He switched on the torch for a second. Eric's ruddy face, a little pale now, stared up at him in the glow. He beckoned, and Eric stole up beside him.

"I'm going on up—with the light off. Don't follow until I tell you."

"Take the gun," Eric said in a low voice. "Or else let me go first."

Traile shook his head. He gripped the handle of the trap-door, then switched off the light. Slowly, the door lifted under his careful pressure. The blackness above for a moment equaled that below. He pushed the door higher, and a faint grayness crept into the dark room above. His anxious gaze made out the blurred outlines of furniture. There was still no sound.

Noiselessly, he drew himself up into the room. The dim light came through crevices in two boarded-up windows at one side. The furniture was covered with bulky canvas, as though the building had been unused for some time. There was no rug on the floor. He tiptoed to the nearest window. Through a crack in the boards he could see a glow, apparently from a street-light.

He tried the door to the next room, opened it an inch. It was dark like the first. As the door swung wider he saw more shrouded furniture. Through a wide connecting doorway he could see into a drawing-room, deserted like the others. Frowning, he went back to the trap-door and called down to Eric in a low voice.

"Come on up. I think we've got the wrong place—but be careful."

He flicked the light on as Eric came up into the room. The brief glow showed a bar for locking the trap. He lowered the door, shoved the bolt in place.

"Just so they can't sneak up on us," he said to Eric. He turned off the light, led the way toward the front of the house. "I'm beginning to think you were right. They must have gone through that other tunnel. Yen Sin never would use a headquarters as vulnerable as this."

"Phew!" said Eric. "I feel a hundred years younger."

"We're still in a bad jam," Traile said grimly. "We'll be arrested as soon as—"

He jumped back, snatching at the dagger. Back in the shadows, one of the chair-covers was slowly lifting into the air!

"Look out, Eric!" he shouted. "Back of you!"

Another ghostly shape was lifting. At his cry of warning, the first chair-cover was tossed into the air. A dark figure sprang at Eric. Traile hurtled between them, savagely struck with the dagger. The dacoit fell to his knees with a bubbling cry. A sibilant voice rasped something from the darkness, and the room seemed suddenly alive with ghostly figures. Eric fired wildly as two of the assassins closed in. One of the men reeled back, but the other knocked the gun from Eric's hand before he could fire again.

A dim blue light spotted Traile. He whirled, poising the bloody dagger. There was a rush of feet from both sides. A chair-cover was whisked down over his head. He struck fiercely through the canvas, felt warm blood spurt onto his hand. Then a violent jerk at the cover threw him to the floor.

A KICK sent him rolling. He brought up against a heavy table with a force that threatened to snap his neck. Voices jabbered in Hindustani, and three or four dacoits pounced on his legs. He was dragged out of the chair-cover, his arms pinioned before he could locate the knife. One of the Burmen seized the dagger, held it at his throat.

The eerie, dark-blue light came closer, rested on his face. Then from behind it came the sibilant voice of Dr. Yen Sin. "You seem to bear a charmed life, Mr. Traile. Or, should I say—to have borne?"

Traile gazed up past the dim light. He could vaguely see the figure of the Crime Emperor. Yen Sin still wore the old Russian uniform, but he had partly removed the astonishing make-up. His black, slanting eyebrows stood out against his high, yellow forehead. The tips of his mandarin mustache, which had been turned in and grayed like the rest, now hung snakily in their normal, jet-black color. Only the false wrinkles in his cheeks remained to hide the full malignancy of his face.

"I hope you will pardon my appearance," the Yellow Doctor said mockingly. "I did not expect the pleasure of this visit."

Traile made no answer. Yen Sin motioned to the dacoits.

"Bind him and place him in the rear room," he ordered. The blue lights shifted, fell on two Chinese and a Hindu who were pinning Eric to the floor. "Bind him, also. Ram Ghar, you will guard them."

"Yes, Master," the dacoit said hastily.

Dr. Yen Sin's tawny eyes looked down at Traile. "You will excuse me?"

The blue light moved away, but in a moment others replaced it as a dozen of Yen Sin's men hurried about in the completion of some task. Traile was tightly bound and carried back into the room with the trap-door. A minute later Eric was brought in, similarly trussed, and swearing fluently. One of the Chinese struck him across the mouth. The two prisoners were laid a few feet apart, and Ram Ghar took up his grim vigil.

The Hindu had placed one of the queer blue lights on an uncovered chair. Traile saw that it was a flashlight with a dark blue lens, evidently intended to keep any glow from being seen through the cracks in the boards. He looked at Eric, and the younger man met his eyes with a crooked grin.

"Well, Michael, I guess its curtains."

Traile winced as he saw that twisted smile. "I'm sorry, old man," he said in a husky voice. "I should have forced you to keep out of this."

Ram Ghar snarled at them in his native tongue.

"The same to you!" retorted Eric.

THE MAN'S hand tightened on his knife. Through the middle room beyond him, Traile could see two of the blue lights bobbing around the drawing-room. A third light suddenly moved toward the rear of the house, then a slender figure in ivory-colored evening gown paused close to the Hindu. As Traile stared up he saw the exotically lovely face of Sonya Damitri.

Her gown was smirched here and there with dirt from the tunnel. One jeweled ear-ring was missing. But as she stood there, the sheen of her dress reflecting the dim light, she was more beautiful than ever. She gazed down at them, her dark, mysterious eyes mirroring a strange expression. Then, abruptly, as her gaze fixed on Eric, her lips curled in a scornful smile.

"Hu-tu dju!" she said, looking back at Ram Ghar. The Hindu grinned and nodded.

"What did she say?" Eric whispered to Traile.

Traile gave the girl an ugly look. "The object of your stubborn admiration called you a stupid pig."

Eric's face slowly reddened. Sonya gave him an odd glance. "I spoke only for the dacoit to hear," she said swiftly, in English. She made a nervous gesture. "Pretend I am threatening you, or he will guess."

Eric's mouth had popped open, but Traile covered up with a fierce glare at the girl. "Go ahead," he snapped impatiently.

She made a pretense of a scornful tirade. "I have a knife in my hand," she said rapidly. "When I push the chair, Ram Ghar's light will roll off to the floor. I'll cut one of you free while he is going after it—or if there is not time, I'll cut the rope so it can be loosened when I attract his attention afterward."

Her dark eyes flashed from Eric to Traile. Ram Ghar looked on, still grinning.

"You are more in the shadow," she told Traile hastily. "I shall cut the rope at your left wrist, and then drop the knife close to your hand. When I get the dacoit's attention, free yourself quickly and then your companion. This side door leads out through the garage."

"What about you?" Eric asked with poorly disguised anxiety.

Traile thought her expressive eyes softened for just an instant. "I can take care of myself," she said in a low voice. Then, aware of the Hindu's gaze, she added in an angry tone, "Be ready! The others will be coming back here in a minute."

Traile looked toward the drawing-room. One of the blue lights was on the floor. Two shadowy forms were bent over, working with something. Sonya moved back, bumped hard against the chair. The dacoit's torch hit the floor, rolled against the baseboard, and went out. The girl hurriedly pointed her own light toward it. As Ram Ghar trotted after the torch, she stooped and slashed at Traile's bonds. The blade cut partly through the loop at his wrist.

Sonya's head was half turned to watch the dacoit. The knife suddenly slipped, grazed Traile's arm. Before she could finish cutting the rope, Ram Ghar stood up with the torch. Helplessly, the girl dropped the knife at Traile's side. He barely had time to hook it in under his elbow as she straightened. Ram Ghar pushed the sliding contact on his flashlight, came back, no longer grinning. He started to growl something at Sonya, but broke off as the precise voice of Dr. Yen Sin came from the drawing-room.

"Work quickly. The cars will be here in five minutes."

A look of despair came into Sonya's face. She slipped back into the gloom, was gone as quickly as she had come. Ram Ghar turned as the Yellow Doctor approached. Yen Sin motioned to him.

"Help them sprinkle the powder."

Traile went cold as he caught Yen Sin's meaning. The Crime Emperor looked down impassively. He had replaced the Russian uniform with his embroidered mandarin robes, and the dim blue light in his hand showed the full evil of the undisguised face above it.

"I regret, Mr. Traile," he said tonelessly, "that I must dispose of you so quickly. You must possess a peculiar brain, to have been so unaffected by my nerve-blocking. I am sorry I have no time to examine it before you join your honorable ancestors."

"You damned fiend!" Eric burst out.

Dr. Yen Sin shrugged. "It is unfortunate, Mr. Gordon, that you have allied yourself with a man who stands in my way."

RAM GHAR and another dacoit came into the room, carrying a long, narrow cylinder. Yen Sin gestured with a yellow claw.

"Encircle our guests," he directed sibilantly.

A stream of black powder was pouring from a hole in one end of the cylinder. The two men made a wide circle enclosing

Traile and Eric. Traile felt beads of perspiration come to his forehead. The Yellow Doctor smiled.

"You are warm, Mr. Traile?"

Traile's bronzed face was grimly set.

"We've lost, Doctor—but you'll never win. Okada will see through the trick in time."

"I am afraid," the Crime Emperor said silkily, "that Okada will have nothing to say about the matter. The secret message which you tried so hard to learn is a copy of a document stolen by my agents in Japan. The Japanese military clique waits only a good excuse to wage war on the United States. My work tonight is the first step in providing that excuse."

He beckoned to a pock-marked Chinese but just as he began an instruction Sonya hurriedly reappeared. Dr. Yen Sin turned. "What is it?" he queried in Chinese.

"A police car has stopped near here," she whispered.

Yen Sin moved his hand, and the blue lights were at once extinguished. One of the men padded to a window and peered out between the close-spaced boards.

"There are only three men, Master. They are not looking at this house."

"The pistol shot was evidently reported by some one in the neighborhood," came the calm response of the Yellow Doctor. "There is little danger of their searching the house, but this forces a change in plans."

"Give me four men, Master," one of the Chinese said eagerly, "and those police will not trouble you."

"There would be gunfire," Yen Sin replied. "Other police

would come, and our cars have not arrived. We will use the exit to the other branch of the tunnel."

Traile heard the men moving around in the darkness. He twisted sidewise, trying to reach the knife. The half-cut rope, which was tied around his body and then looped at his wrists, dug hard into his flesh.

"Open the trap and lower the dispatch box," the unruffled voice of Dr. Yen Sin came from the dark. "Sonya, you will follow Ling Ho."

The girl made an anxious plea in an undertone. The Yellow Doctor coldly replied, cutting her short. In a few moments the footsteps and whispers faded away, but Traile knew the trap had not closed. He was striving to work the knife into his fingers when a match suddenly flared up. He froze. Just above the trap showed the malignant face of Dr. Yen Sin. He moved the match toward the train of powder.

"Good-bye, Mr. Traile," he said softly. "I am sorry I cannot be with you in your last moments."

There was a flash as the powder lit up. The Yellow Doctor vanished, and the trap thudded shut. With a low roar, the fire raced along the path of black powder, starting to circle the room. The leaping flame caught at a canvas chair cover, swept on to the other rooms.

TRAILE'S HAND had closed convulsively on the knife. He jerked onto his side, twisting the blade toward the nearest strand of rope. It was almost touching when his cramped fingers dropped the knife. With a groan, he lunged after it. The flame on his side of the room had set fire to the wood work, was mounting toward the ceiling. He heard Eric cry out something, but there was no time to look. With all his might, he threw himself toward the knife. He fell short, but with a snap the half-severed rope broke under the sudden strain.

His left hand was instantly freed. He seized the knife, rolled away from the spreading flames. It was but the work of a second to cut the bonds at his feet. He sprang up, tearing the other loop from his right hand. Eric was struggling madly to free himself. Traile slashed the ropes at Eric's feet, swiftly helped him up.

"The trap!" he shouted hoarsely.

"Wait—there's a break in the flames!" Eric yelled.

Traile stumbled after him as he ploughed into the smoke. One whole side of the room was on fire, and the terrific heat seemed about to engulf them both. But in a second the roar of the flames lessened, and with a gasp of relief he felt cool air in his lungs. Eric clutched at him, pulled him along.

"We're in the garage she told us about!" he said thickly. "Now if we can find the door—"

He bumped against it as he spoke. Traile helped him slide it back, and they plunged out into the welcome coolness of the night.

"Keep going," Traile muttered. "We don't want those police to catch us."

They dodged around a vine-covered trellis, found concealment behind a thick hedge at the rear of the grounds. They crouched there, gazing back. Smoke and flame poured from the lower windows of the house, and in another minute the entire structure was a mass of fire. Traile saw a uniformed figure run around the rear, then another policeman appeared from the other side. Lights were flashing on in nearby houses, and in another minute the shriek of sirens announced the approach of fire-engines.

"We'd better get away before they see us," Traile told Eric.

They stole into an alley, hurried along in the deepest shadow. Four blocks away, midway of another alley, they halted and stared at each other.

"That gap in the flames?" Traile asked, curiously. "Was that Sonya's work?"

Eric quickly nodded. "I saw her brush the powder with her foot. She must have done most of it after the lights were put out."

"I was wrong about her," Traile said slowly.

Eric's youthful face tightened. "He must have some terrible hold over her."

Traile gave him a searching glance.

"Be careful, Eric," he said gravely. "She's still a tool of Dr. Yen Sin."

CHAPTER 11
THE MAN WITH THE SCAR

AT ONE side of a peculiar switchboard, which had been installed horizontally in the center of a map of Washington, a tiny purple light suddenly flashed. The tawny, slanting eyes of the man at the table impassively shifted to a corresponding circle on an adjacent strip of the map. His long hand reached out from the flowing sleeve of his silken mandarin robe, and one sharp-nailed finger moved a toggle switch.

"Report," came the emotionless command of the Invisible Emperor.

There was a pause, then a man's nervous voice spoke from the ebony box on the table. "Number Sixty-nine. I am calling for instructions about tonight."

The eyes of the Yellow Doctor narrowed slightly. "You were directed to follow the same procedure as of Wednesday last."

"I am afraid to go that way," the unseen man said tensely. "I believe they suspect something."

Dr. Yen Sin pressed a button at the lower edge of the switch-board, and a needle at once quivered on a small dial beside the button. As he watched it, the pupils of his eyes dwindled to pin-points.

"Your instructions are altered," he said tonelessly. "It is now thirty minutes past seven. In exactly one hour, you will leave the Mayflower Hotel. You will walk north to Dupont Circle, making sure you are not followed. As you start eastward around the circle, a Sunshine taxicab will draw up near you. You will enter. The woman in the cab will give you further orders. Is this clear?"

"Yes, I understand perfectly," came the hasty reply from the box. "I was only—"

"That is all," said Dr. Yen Sin. He disconnected the switch, and the purple light went out. His weird eyes rested for an instant on the dial, then he touched another switch. A green light glowed.

"*Tchee*, Master?" a reedy voice answered in Chinese.

"A special order concerning Number Sixty-nine," said the Yellow Doctor calmly. He spoke for several moments…. "Alive, if possible."

The green light went out. For a minute the board was dark, the room silent. The Crime Emperor sat unmoving, his half-closed eyes fixed in space.

Suddenly the teletype ticker at the other end of the table rattled into action. The Yellow Doctor stood up, read the printed words as they were clicked off on the tape. His pointed eyebrows slowly drew together. As the ticker went silent, he resumed his seat. He traced down the left-hand strip of the divided map, shifted a toggle beside a red circle. But the ebony box was still. FOR TWENTY minutes, he sat there, waiting. Other lights flashed. He pressed a button each time, and the lights disappeared as they were answered at some other spot. Then, abruptly, the ebony box gave forth a loud click. Dr. Yen Sin leaned forward.

"Who did you say?" a brusque voice demanded.

"A Mr. Barnes, sir—he said you asked him to phone," said another speaker.

"Put him on—and don't break in for anybody," snapped the first man.

There was another click, then a cautious voice spoke. "I want to speak to Mr. Glover."

The yellow hand on the toggle switch tightened.

"It's all right, Eric," came the lowered voice of the F.B.I. director. "This is Glover talking. Where are you?"

He seized the yellow
man's pigtail.

"Seventh and H Streets," said Eric hastily, "right on the edge of Chinatown. I was to meet Michael at—"

"Wait," cut in Glover, "are you sure no one can hear you?"

"Yes, this is the only phone booth," Eric's reply echoed from the ebony box. "Listen, something's happened. I've missed Michael—but I saw the Vaughan girl."

"What?" rasped Glover.

"She was getting out of a car, a block from here. I was sneaking through an alley and I—"

Dr. Yen Sin reached out and pressed a red button. Eric's words were still sounding from the amplifier-box.

"I don't see yet how she gave me the slip. I know she went into one of those shops—"

"By God, somebody'll catch it for this!" Glover's words rasped from the box. "I had two men watching the British Embassy to nab her. Raville had it almost arranged for them to turn her over to us."

The pock-marked face of Ling Ho appeared in the light of the tilted reflector beyond the table. Dr. Yen Sin wrote on a pad, handed him the message. Ling Ho stared in amazement at the words, then hurried out to the arched vestibule and vanished.

"—have to be careful," Glover was saying tautly. "The police still think those two burned bodies were yours and Michael's, and they've got to keep thinking that till this is cleared up. I can't come there myself—I'm due at a conference in thirty minutes; Ambassador Okada is coming here, and we're going to try to prove that Dr. Yen Sin worked the whole thing."

"What'll I do?" Eric asked anxiously.

"Go down Seventh to G Street. Wait on the north side of G Street between there and Eighth. Jack Fowler and a squad will be there in ten minutes. Take them where you saw Iris Vaughan."

The ebony box clicked. Instantly, the yellow hand of the Crime Emperor swept out toward the massed switches before him. His long fingers moved with the precision of an automaton.

A light flashed, then another, and a third. Calmly, Dr. Yen Sin began to speak.

THE SEEDY, furtive man who stood before the window of Hai Yung's curio shop had the look of a sailor who had served in tropical seas. His hollow face had a dark, leathery color, and about his eyes were deep-etched lines as though from long hours of squinting under a brassy sun. A ragged scar twisted one side of his mouth, creating an ugly leer.

He stood with his head stuck forward, his ill-fitting coat bunched across his shoulders. His black hair was awry under a greasy cap. At a glance, he was distinctly foreign, with an evil look which could not be disguised.

A car rolled past, stopped before the adjoining Chinese shop. A man and a woman stepped out, disappeared within the building. The scarred man looked after them with a trace of curiosity, then resumed his study of the window. He fished a cigarette from his pocket with a grimy hand, sniffed it, put it back. With a careful glance up and down the street, he entered the shop.

A middle-aged Chinese with a bland, expressionless face, started around from behind a display case. His black eyes flitted over the other man's seedy coat, came back to the scarred face. "You wish something?" he said with only a hint of accent.

The scarred man slowly closed one eye in a wink. "Kang Po—Pell Street—Number Nineteen," he said hoarsely. "And don't worry about the cash—I ain't as poor as I look."

For just a second, the Chinese looked frightened.

"You make mistake," he said.

"Don't come none o' that," said the other, roughly. He produced the limp cigarette. "Here, if you got to be so careful. Take a smell—and there's the joss-mark."

His voice was rising. The Chinese looked anxiously toward the door. "You come back—not tonight," he whispered. "Maybe tomorrow—"

The scarred mouth pulled into a snarl. "Tomorrow'll be too late. I got to have it now. And don't tell me you ain't catchem pipe—"

"Yes, yes—all right, please," the Chinese said hastily. Two or three passersby were looking in from the street. Beyond them, a strolling policeman had paused. The merchant caught at his unwelcome visitor's arm. "You come—I show you better necklace for lady," he said in a loud voice.

The policeman sauntered on, and the scarred man followed the unhappy merchant into a rear room. Another Chinese, younger, skinny, and wearing huge tortoise-shell glasses, stood up quickly from a desk wedged between stacks of merchandise. The two Orientals whispered in their own language, then the skinny one hurried into the front of the shop. The other had partly recovered his bland appearance.

"You wait—I bring here," he said. But the scarred man scowled, lapsed further into pidgin dialect.

"Where t'hell I smokum?" he demanded. "No hab pipe—you catchem safe place for dream trip. Two—three pipe, and I gotchee plenty Dutch gold."

He brought out two shining coins, clinked them together. The merchant's eyes gleamed, then fear came back into their depths. He hesitated, then closed and locked the door leading to the front. Beckoning, he led the way to basement steps. They went down into a room cluttered with still more merchandise, boxes, and Chinese furniture. The Oriental pushed against the side of a table. It lifted, raising a hinged door to which it was firmly attached. The scarred man followed down into a narrow passage. His guide slapped his hand against a spot on the wall, and in a moment a heavy door, with hinges and lock hidden on the reverse side, opened surreptitiously. The merchant spoke in Cantonese, and a dim light went on. It revealed a thick-set, pigtailed Chinese, and back of him a row of bunks, double-tiered. There was no one else in sight.

A QUICK look passed between the two yellow men. With a few hasty words in Chinese, the merchant withdrew. The pigtailed Oriental closed and barred the heavy door. He pointed to one of the bunks.

"You gettum ready. I fix pipe."

The scarred man sat down on the edge of the bunk, gazed about the shadowy room. The other bunks were empty.

"What t'hell, Charlie?" he grumbled. "Nobody else catchee tonight?"

The Chinese did not answer. He had lighted a spirit lamp, was holding a tiny ball of opium near the blue flame. He moved it back and forth, then pushed the glowing bit of drug into the brass bowl of a small pipe he had already heated. With an oblique glance, he went to the bunk, extended the pipe.

The scarred man took it, still grumbling. He waited until the pigtailed one had gone back to a chair in the shadows. Then he slid back, one leg dangling over the edge of the bunk. Tossing his cap aside, he raised the pipe to his lips.

Five minutes passed. The man's intermittent complaints died away. He mumbled a request for a second pipe, but the first one slipped from his fingers even as he spoke. His dark eyes closed. The Chinese waited five minutes more, then tiptoed toward the bunk. From somewhere behind him, a dull, metallic boom faintly sounded. He stiffened, but the man in the bunk did not move. Silently, he bent over the sprawled figure, and reached into the man's coat pocket. He took the gold coins, then gripped the wooden rail which projected above the mattress.

The bunk began to tilt. It had hardly moved when with incredible speed the scarred man leaped up. His dangling leg hooked the edge of the bunk, and his hands shot around the pigtailed one's throat. The Oriental let go the bunk, tore wildly at the fingers compressing his windpipe. The scarred man held on grimly.

The frantic struggles of the Chinese threw him against the wooden rail. The bunk canted steeply, and the other man's fingers were almost torn from their grip. His right hand flicked out, seized the yellow man's pigtail. In a twinkling, it was looped around its owner's throat. The ill-fated Celestial thrashed backward in a frenzied attempt to break free. As he slumped to the floor, the bunk came back to level. The scarred man rolled out, his dark hands relentlessly tightening the pigtail.

A few more seconds, and the Chinese lay motionless, his tongue protruding from his blackened lips. The other man released his hold. Turning, he pressed against the bunk. It tilted as before, disclosing a precipitous slide which ended in a small, black dungeon. He nodded grimly to himself. That fall would have been enough to kill him. It was a good thing he had understood their words.

He lifted the dead Chinese, rolled him into the bunk and down the slide. The body struck with a sickening thud at the bottom. He closed the bunk, straightened the rumpled blanket. Taking his cap, he moved silently to the rear of the room. That muffled gong had seemed to come from somewhere not far away. He found a door similar to the one through which he had entered, and after listening for a minute, carefully unbarred it. It opened into a small closet, at the other end of which was an ordinary door.

He stepped inside, pulling the secret door shut. There was no sound from beyond the closet. He opened the other door an inch or two, peered out. The room was like a small chamber in some unimportant Chinese joss-house. Punk-sticks were smoldering on both sides of a huge idol which reposed on a pedestal. Prayer-mats covered the floor.

The scarred man was about to steal out of the closet when footsteps sounded from the left. He hastily drew back, leaving the door open enough so that he could see through the crack. His right hand gripped a gun he had taken from under his coat.

An old Chinese, thin and shriveled, came into view. He was followed by another Oriental—a lean, sinewy man—who was guiding a white man by the arm. The one he was guiding was dressed in evening clothes, and a heavy blindfold covered his eyes. The uncovered part of his face was pale and drawn.

THE OLD Chinese stopped before the huge joss. Reaching up a wizened hand, he pressed the idol's staring left eye. With a faint grating, the joss swung open, revealing a shadowy passage on the other side. The younger Chinese stepped through, piloting the white man. The older Oriental touched the right eye of the idol, and the joss swung shut. Muttering to himself, he went back the way he had come.

The man in the closet took a step toward the joss, then looked down at his clothes. Moving back, he quickly brought a small, flat leather packet from the inner pocket of his coat. It opened into a tiny make-up kit. He propped it up on a shelf, and switched on a pencil flashlight. Pouring alcohol onto a pad, he swiped at the ragged scar. It vanished. He poured a greaseless liquid from another small bottle, and vigorously wiped his face. The hollows disappeared from his cheeks, leaving them merely lean. In another moment the deep squint-lines were gone, and in place of the scarred sailor's features was the alert, tanned face of Michael Traile.

Swiftly, he cleaned his grimy hands, then combed his hair. He threw away the greasy cap, took off his coat and discarded the towel which had made the lumps at his shoulders. He brushed the dust from his lapels, pulled at the sleeves and partly removed the wrinkles. As he put on the coat, he took a final glance into the mirror in his kit.

There was danger now, but even more if he had kept the disguise. The scarred sailor would be noticed at once, even in the other role he was planning. There was no time for building up another face, and a careless change would be worse than none.

He put away the kit, took his gun and closed the door back of him. He reached the joss, pressed the left eye. It slid, and the idol began to open. He jumped to the other side, but no one was visible in the passage. The light from the room vaguely showed a narrow cross-walk of planks, extending over the blackness of an old sewer. On the other side, he could see where the path turned to the left.

He wheeled, tugged at the joss. It moved reluctantly, started to close. Suddenly, a crouching form stirred in the shadow back of the idol.

"*Ho ren?*" came a fierce challenge.

Traile spun around in consternation. There stood Ram Ghar!

Amazement shot into the dacoit's brown face as he saw the man he had thought dead. Traile leaped. Ram Ghar sprang back, jerking his knife from his belt. Traile's finger moved on his trigger, then in a split-second change of mind he whirled the pistol upward. With a vicious crunch, the butt struck Ram Ghar's head. The dacoit's snarl broke in a groan. He tottered back, still clenching his knife. Then a rotting guard-rail gave way, and he plunged headlong into the sewer.

Traile stared down at the dark waters as the dacoit's body was borne off by that evil tide. There was no sound from the doomed man, only the ugly gurgle of the sewer. He shook off the brief nausea which had swept over him, and turned as the idol grated shut.

A thin, vertical line of light was showing close to where Ram Ghar had stood. He lifted his automatic, crept forward. Then he saw that the light came from between the doors of a cabinet placed against the moldy stone wall. He took a quick look inside. At least twenty blindfolds hung on numbered pegs. There were several other pegs on which he saw half-length masks of gray cloth, with elastic cords.

HE TOOK one of the masks and closed the cabinet doors. It was evident that certain members of the Invisible Empire had been halted here, and their blindfolds exchanged for the masks, probably to keep their identity unknown to other members. These would be the unwilling agents of Dr. Yen Sin, he swiftly surmised as he started along the narrow cross-walk. If he only knew whether the masks were later removed....

He stopped. A hundred feet away, in the darkness along the path, a flashlight was spotting the ground as someone approached. With noiseless steps, he reached the other side of the sewer, flattened himself against the arched brickwork. The light came closer, and he saw the sinewy Chinese who had guided the blindfolded man. The Oriental's head was bent, his eyes on the path. He was almost to Traile when he swung the light to locate the narrow bridge. The rays fell on Traile's feet.

Traile sprang, poked his gun into the man's ribs. Terror raced into the Oriental's eyes.

"Tan-dz!" he groaned.

"Right—I'm a spy!" Traile said coldly. "And you'll be a corpse if you make just one wrong move!"

The flashlight was shaking in the guide's grasp. Traile drew the gray mask over his face.

"Lead the way," he ordered. "You're taking me where you took the others."

The Chinese turned gray with horror. "No, no!" he moaned. "He will kill me!"

Traile spun him around. "You've one chance to live—do what I tell you!"

Visibly quaking, the Oriental led him to where the path entered a break in the arched wall. Traile stopped him. "What's on the other side?" he demanded in a low tone.

"Another path," the Chinese said, looking fearfully over his shoulder.

"Then what?"

"A—a door," whimpered his captive. "They will kill me—and you, too—if I take you in there."

"How many guards at that door?" Traile said curtly.

"Two—and two more inside," replied the frightened Oriental.

Traile rammed his gun a little harder into the man's back. "We're going ahead. I'm another member of the Invisible Empire you're bringing in. The number of this mask is Eighty-three, if they ask who I am."

The other's shoulders sagged, but he went on. They passed through the break in the arch, followed a curving path. They were almost at the end when voices sounded from somewhere on the right. A rectangle of light appeared, as a narrow door opened. Traile cast a quick glance that way, saw a second path leading away under the gloomy, vaulted roof.

Two gunmen were hustling a short, brown-faced man in through the doorway. The prisoner's hands were tied behind his back, and his mouth was tightly gagged. As the two white men jerked the captive inside, his glaring face showed in the light. Traile barely stifled an exclamation. The prisoner was Ambassador Okada!

CHAPTER 12
THE ONYX POOL

THE DOOR closed, and only the glow of the Chinaman's flashlight broke the utter blackness. Traile followed the man, fighting against a new despair. It had been bad enough before this perilous quest for proof of America's innocence—as well as Eric's and his own—in the Embassy outrage. But now, with Okada kidnapped, and by white men....

"Lee ding!" a guttural voice came from the darkness. Traile slipped his gun into his coat pocket, pressed the muzzle against the side of his guide.

"I am bringing Number Eighty-three," the Chinese spoke up hastily. "He was questioned by Ah Fong, and his photograph checked."

The writhing hand sank as the guards brought in Eric Gordon.

The guttural voice grunted, and a dim blue light shone above a slowly opening door. Two fierce-looking Chinese stared at Traile as he went in at his guide's elbow. A black curtain moved aside, and two more armed Orientals appeared. They gave him only a scant inspection, noting his guide, then looked back at something they had been watching.

Traile stole a glance about him. They had entered a weird, circular room. Lights slanted from several angles shone down on a strange assemblage. At one side were twelve or fifteen men and a smaller group of women wearing gray half-masks. Some were in evening clothes, some in street attire. The men were bare-headed. All of the group were Caucasians. To the other side, and unmasked, was a motley crowd of Chinese, Malays, and Hindus, bringing up the total number to forty or more. A veiled slave-girl in Oriental costume stood beside heavy velvet portières on the right.

On a platform at the opposite side from which he stood, Traile saw a large, fantastic chair upon a dais. The chair was gilded, and coiled about the back and the arms was an enormous serpent carved and painted so perfectly that it seemed to be alive. Stretching away on both sides of the dais were tapestries which reached up to the shadowy ceiling. The chair was empty.

Though there were at least sixty people within the circular room, there was not a word spoken. Only the faint rustle of women's gowns, the sound of nervously shifted feet, broke the stillness. A sweet, cloying incense filled the air, and after a moment Traile realized that it held some subtle drug. The faces of the nearest Orientals had a dull, fixed look. Their eyes never left the golden serpent chair on the dais.

Even Traile's unwilling guide seemed to be falling under the spell of that mysterious incense. He ceased to tremble, and his fear-stiffened face gradually relaxed into a blank stare. Traile pushed him ahead, seeking the darkest part of the room.

Suddenly, a deep-tone gong boomed out a resonant signal. Its thunder echoed throughout the circular room, swelling, returning in slow waves of sound. It was a full minute before the last low thunder died away. There was an almost dreadful silence. Traile found himself staring like the rest at the center of the motionless tapestries, where the glittering eyes of the serpent seemed to watch the assemblage.

Slowly, the lights faded. The painted serpent lost its hideous outlines, became a shadow. The lights went out, and a complete hush left. Then an amber glow shone from some hidden source. And there on the dais, like some grim and ominous statue, sat Dr. Yen Sin!

Under that pallid light, his yellow mandarin robes blended with the golden chair so flat he seemed to be a part of it,—with the hideous serpent coiled about him. In his left hand was a queer, sardonic mask, like a caricature of his own face. The amber light was slanted from above so that his features were in shadow. The effect was indescribably terrible. It was as though that motionless figure had removed his face and held it out before him, leaving a sinister blackness where it had been.

FOR A moment the tension was almost unendurable. Traile found himself wanting to shout, to make some violent move-

ment—anything to break that awful hush. Then suddenly he knew what had happened to him. On all but him, that subtle drug had had its effect, had stupefied their minds, leaving them easy prey to the uncanny power of the man in the serpent chair.

But in his sleepless brain there had been no subtle deadening.

Dr. Yen Sin whirled and threw Sonya before him.

Instead, a nervous tension was growing—a swift up-building of energy—some odd reaction to that unknown drug. He set his jaw, battling to hold himself in. To let go now would be fatal.

Dr. Yen Sin raised his right hand from the scaly coils of the serpent. A jeweled shield gleamed on his index finger. An enormously long fingernail, such as once marked the royalty of China, extended from the shield so that it seemed to be part of his finger. As he moved his hand, the amber light was at once shifted so that it shone more brightly on the hushed assemblage. Traile felt as though he stood nakedly before the searching eyes of the Yellow Doctor.

Then a kneeling Chinese before the dais spoke a singsong phrase in mandarin dialect. Dr. Yen Sin answered with a gesture. The Chinese stood up, spoke sharply to men waiting at the right A curved door slid into a niche, and two Orientals in native costume appeared, bringing a third figure between them.

For an instant, Traile thought it was Okada. Then he saw that it was a white man. The prisoner was unmasked. His plump face was ashen, and but for the two Chinese he would have fallen to the floor. The group nearest the spot fell back as he was brought in, and for the first time Traile saw a peculiar, black mirror just in front of the dais. It was about eight feet square, and under the amber glow it shone like polished onyx.

The Chinese guards halted at one side of the black square, facing Dr. Yen Sin. The Yellow Doctor slowly lowered the gargoyle mask. To Traile, his shadowed face was only a blur, but to that trembling wretch before the dais he knew it must be like a nightmare. For almost a minute, Yen Sin fixedly regarded the man before him. The silence was like that of a tomb.

"You will stand—alone," came the toneless voice of the Crime Emperor.

The guards quickly stepped away. The prisoner stood as though turned to stone.

The emotionless voice went on.

"Number Sixty-nine, you have been accused of treason against the Invisible Empire. The specific offense is that of attempting to assist police officials in tracing a message to enable them to locate this headquarters. What is your answer?"

"They had been hounding me—I was insane from the third degree!" the accused man burst out wildly. "For God's sake, give me another chance!"

The Yellow Doctor sat back, his right hand slowly caressing the coils of the serpent.

"My answer lies in the mirror beside you."

The white man turned and gazed at the polished black surface. He shook his head blankly. "But I see nothing."

The long fingernail pointed. "Step closer."

The white man took a stumbling step. Back in the shadows, Traile stared at that shining black square.

"Closer," came the inexorable voice from the dais.

Like a man in a dream, the traitor obeyed. His faltering steps took him to the edge. He paused, looking down at his reflection. As though it were a magnet, he dazedly moved onward. His feet touched the gleaming black surface.

A strange movement swept the surface of the onyx-like square. On the instant, it became a pool of quivering black slime. A terrible scream burst from the traitor's throat. He made a frenzied attempt to leap back, but his feet were already sinking into that black morass.

A WAVE of horror swept over the gray-masked group. A woman cried out in a choked voice. From up on the dais, the mask of Dr. Yen Sin sardonically smiled down.

Scream after scream rang through the room as the doomed

137

man sank to his death. Slowly, the black ooze rose about him. With a shriek, he raised both arms in wild supplication to the man in the serpent chair. Dr. Yen Sin did not move.

Sick with horror, Traile tore his eyes away. There was a moment when the insane cries of the dying man almost sent him dashing forward, though he knew it would be useless. Then a terrible moan ended those pitiful shrieks, and he knew that it was over.

In spite of himself, his eyes went back to that deadly pool. A shudder swept over him, as he saw a writhing hand sink down into the ooze. He jerked his glance aside. The Chinese guards were bringing in another prisoner. He took one look, then his heart almost stood still.

It was Eric Gordon!

Half-dazed, he saw the two Chinese drag Eric before the dais. Eric was struggling fiercely to break the twisting hold of his guards. Dr. Yen Sin leaned forward, pointing toward the black pool.

"We will waste no time with this man," he said coldly.

The two Chinese hauled Eric toward the death-pit. Traile snatched out his gun, sprang forward, one hand at his mask. His guide suddenly gave a shout of warning. A Malay charged into Traile's path. Traile hurled him aside, took swift aim at one of the guards.

Flame spurted from the pistol, and the Chinese fell back with a groan. Eric sent the other man headlong with a furious uppercut. Dr. Yen Sin was on his feet, his hand raised in a swift signal. The amber light narrowed into a dazzling beam, swerved to spot Traile. He jumped to one side. A dacoit's clutching hands shot toward his throat. He drilled the Hindu through the head, then hastily lifted the gun. The glowing amber eye was probing after him. He fired straight at it. There was a double report, and the chamber was plunged into darkness.

Eric's white-clad figure was a vague blur just ahead. Traile dropped his mask, sprang and caught Eric's arm.

"It's Michael!" he shouted above the din. They dashed around the dais platform. Blue flashlights lit up at a dozen points.

"Look!" Eric said tensely. Traile whirled. Twenty feet away, another curved door had opened. As they dashed through it, a slender form was visible inside the opening.

"Sonya!" cried Eric.

She hastily locked the curved door, her face deathly pale.

"Quick—follow me!" she whispered. She thrust a gun into Eric's hand.

They ran through a passage, and into a luxuriously furnished room, where a Chandu layout stood before a cushion-strewn divan. A blond woman jumped to her feet, and Traile recognized Iris Vaughan. Her eyes were dilated from opium.

"Bring her with you," Sonya said hurriedly. The other girl shrank back, but Traile drew her along. They entered a long chamber fitted as a chemical laboratory. In a recess, a dead man sat rigidly upright on an operating-table. His face was yellow, distorted.

"The Dragon's Shadow!" Eric said hoarsely.

Sonya Damitri shivered. "No," she said in a low voice, "that is but one of the ways death comes to those who stand in the Shadow of the Dragon."

"Where is Okada?" Traile asked tautly, as she turned to a steel door.

"I don't know," she whispered. "It would be madness to search for him. You must escape at once."

"You've got to come with us!" Eric said desperately.

"My father is held prisoner at Yen Sin's base in China," she replied in a hopeless voice. "If I fled, he would die a terrible death."

ERIC GROANED. A strange, sad smile came to her lips, but it abruptly vanished. For as the steel door began to open, voices were audible.

"But, Master, there are a hundred agents and police! They are searching every store in Chinatown!"

The voice of Dr. Yen Sin replied calmly. "Follow my orders. There is no great danger, unless those two escape. In an emergency, we will abandon these headquarters according to plan."

Sonya had stepped back, her finger at her lips. Before Traile could prevent it, Iris Vaughan gave a scream. A chair grated sharply within the room. Traile hurled himself against the steel door, locked it and spun the dial.

"Back to the first room!" Sonya said in a moan.

Eric had one hand clasped over the blond girl's mouth. She threw him off angrily as they reached the luxurious Chandu cell. Sonya faced her, with her dark eyes flashing.

"Little fool! I was only trying to save your life. *He* means to kill you, now that you can serve him no longer."

"You're lying!" cried Iris Vaughan, but her face was suddenly haggard.

Jabbered words in Chinese became audible from the other end of the passage. Sonya ran to the red and gold screen against the wall. She swung it aside, beckoned for Eric to help her. A block of stone rotated silently, leaving an aperture about five feet high.

"Only Yen Sin and the man with whom he was talking know this place," she said in an undertone. "Wait inside! I shall open it when the guards have searched this room."

Traile was the last one through. He tugged on an iron ring, and the stone closed. He had expected black silence, but instead a faint, monotonous hissing was audible, and from somewhere nearby he saw a dim, green light. It shone through a thin, dark curtain, silhouetting several dancing figurines.

Just inside the curtain was a large teakwood chair. On the other side was a room devoid of windows or doors. Tapestries and prints covered the walls. Two or three sets of small Chinese gongs hung down on silken cords. The pale green light came from the eyes and nostrils of a huge brass dragon lamp fastened to the ceiling.

Traile took a cautious step after Eric and Iris Vaughan. Then he went rigid, as they had done. For there at one side, just visible in the emerald light, was Dr. Yen Sin!

For a second, Traile was dumbfounded. Only a few moments before, he had heard the Crime Emperor in that other room. But it was certainly Yen Sin. He was bending over, securing the triple locks on a small brass-bound box which stood on a tabaret. With a start, Traile recognized it from Okada's description of the stolen dispatch-box.

Suddenly, the Yellow Doctor turned, and his tawny eyes passed over the black curtain. Iris Vaughan gave a frightened cry. Before Yen Sin could move, Traile leaped between the curtains, lifting his gun.

"Raise your hands!" he rasped.

A bare instant, murder shone in the yellow face before him. Then with a curious, mocking smile, Dr. Yen Sin obeyed.

"Your ability to surprise, Mr. Traile, is quite remarkable," he said suavely. "But I see you had a charming assistant."

"No, no!" Iris Vaughan cried wildly. "They forced me to do this!"

Dr. Yen Sin slowly moved his head.

"You may explain to Ling Ho, when he arrives."

Eric was covering him from the other side. "Just try one yell—" he began fiercely. But Traile sprang to the teakwood chair.

"He's warned them already! There's a tiny Dictaphone recessed here in the back! It caught everything."

Eric swore. "That's why we thought he was in that room!"

A muffled pounding rose above the ceaseless hiss of the green-eyed dragon. Men were tapping the walls.

"Glover's agents!" exclaimed Traile. "Tear down that Indian print! We'll signal back!"

Eric yanked down the print, revealing the barren stone. Suddenly Yen Sin stepped backward. Both Eric and Traile lunged after him. A diabolical smile had come into the Yellow Doctor's face. Traile hastily looked about them. Then a cold chill raced up his spine.

All but Yen Sin were in the dragon's shadow!

HE SHOT a look upward. Yen Sin's hand had closed on the tassel of one of the gongs. A frightful premonition swept over Traile. But even as he leaped, that yellow claw jerked the cord.

The dragon's hiss rose to a sudden rambling. Green flame shot from its nostrils. Then with a roar, its jaws flashed open. Down into the room belched a scorching emerald fire—the deadly green flame of the piercing death!

In his frantic leap, Traile hurtled into Eric. Eric slid to the floor beyond the blast of fire. A terrific heat whirled out after Traile as he dived to safety. He had a glimpse of Iris Vaughan, huddled back against the wall. As he jumped up, he saw the Yellow Doctor spring toward the teakwood chair.

A claw-like hand jabbed at the oval box on one arm, and the flaming dragon swiftly began to turn. Cracked mortar flew in all directions as the green fire swept over the wall toward the two Americans. Shading his eyes, Traile raced toward Dr. Yen Sin.

The Crime Emperor whirled. Traile drove him back at gunpoint, flung a swift look toward the wall. The powerful chemical flame was almost in the center. He felt over the top of the oval box. One switch-button protruded. He pressed it, and the dragon ceased to move. Eric dashed toward him.

"Cover Yen Sin!" Traile clipped at him. He jumped toward the gong tassel, as with a sudden grinding the green flame pierced the wall. A spring release took effect as he jerked at the cord, and the green fire quickly faded. Excited voices sounded outside, and in a moment uniformed police and G-Men were crowding at the hole.

"Hurry up!" shouted Traile. "We've captured Dr. Yen Sin!"

There was a stifled cry. He spun around. Sonya's white face was gazing from the darkness back of the chair. Eric's eyes twitched toward her. Yen Sin's hand instantly shot out and Eric went tumbling to the floor. With incredible swiftness, the Yellow Doctor whirled and threw Sonya before him. He jumped backward. There was a whistling sound, and a dense black cloud whirled about the chair.

Half a minute later, as the G-Men's torches stabbed through the thinning smoke. Traile hastily searched the room. Dr. Yen Sin had vanished. Iris Vaughan lay on the floor in a faint. Of Sonya, there was no sign, but he saw that the secret stone was open.

"Where is he?" demanded a familiar voice.

Traile turned, saw Glover's excited face. He grimaced. "I spoke too soon."

Glover barked a command, and his agents spread out in hasty search. In a few minutes he returned to report "He's gone—and all but some small fry," he growled. "But, thank God, we've saved Okada. And with this dispatch-box, that settles the Japanese Embassy affair. But damned if I see how Yen Sin got out of here."

Traile was bending over the floor by the chair. He stood up, pressed one button after another in the top of the oval box. Without a sound, the chair suddenly sank down into a square shaft. Eric and Glover stared over his shoulder as he knelt with a flashlight.

Stretching away below was the evil blackness of the old sewer. On the narrow platform where the chair rested was a yellow mandarin hat, its plumes dangling in the slime. The darkly flowing water was the only sign of life.

"By God!" exclaimed Glover. "He drowned himself when he saw he was finished."

Eric's blue eyes lit with a quick relief.

"Michael, that means Sonya will be free!"

Traile stood up, his bronzed face sober. He slowly shook his head. "I'm afraid that the Dragon's Shadow has not gone forever," he mused.

POPULAR PUBLICATIONS
HERO PULPS

LOOK FOR MORE SOON!

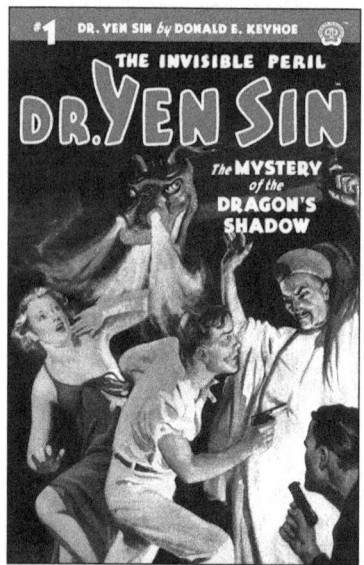

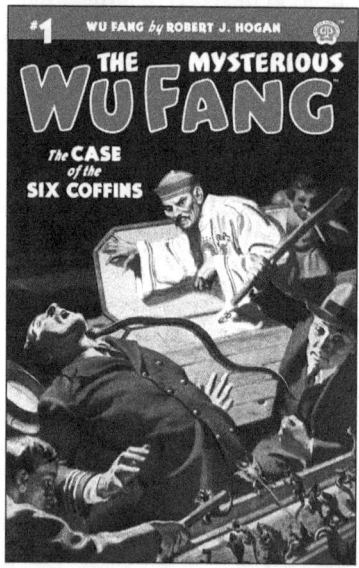